ADVANCE PRAISE FOR
I'LL LIVE

"Stephen Manes has made a strong, deeply moving, and life-centered novel from one of the hardest of individual—and family—situations. I'LL LIVE faces up squarely to agonizing questions and all their emotional and ethical paradoxes. With the book's bright qualities, however, there is no final sense of despair but, rather, love and courage; not a story of how we choose to die, but how we choose to live."

LLOYD ALEXANDER
Winner of The American Book Award and
The Newbery Medal

I'LL LIVE

Stephen Manes

AN AVON  FLARE BOOK

I'LL LIVE is an original publication of Avon Books. This work has never before appeared in book form.

The lines from "Buffalo Bill 's" are reprinted from TULIPS & CHIMNEYS by e. e. cummings, by permission of Liveright Publishing Corporation. Copyright 1923, 1925 and renewed 1951, 1953 by e. e. cummings. Copyright © 1973, 1976 by Nancy T. Andrews. Copyright © 1973, 1976 by George James Firmage.

AVON BOOKS
A division of
The Hearst Corporation
959 Eighth Avenue
New York, New York 10019

Copyright © 1982 by Stephen Manes
Published by arrangement with the author
Library of Congress Catalog Card Number: 82-11538
ISBN: 0-380-81737-3

Library of Congress Cataloging in Publication Data
Manes, Stephen, 1949-
    I'll live.
    (An Avon/Flare book)
    Summary: Eighteen-year-old Dylan faces painful changes brought on by his father's terminal illness.
    [1. Fathers and sons—Fiction. 2. Death—Fiction]
I. Title.
PZ7.M31264Il 1982   [Fic]   82-11538
ISBN: 0-380-81737-3

First Flare Printing, November, 1982

FLARE BOOKS TRADEMARK REG. U. S. PAT. OFF. AND IN
OTHER COUNTRIES, MARCA REGISTRADA, HECHO EN U. S. A.

Printed in the U. S. A.

WFH 10 9 8 7 6 5 4 3 2 1

for Dad

he was a handsome man

                     and what i want to know is
how do you like your blueeyed boy
Mister Death

                 — e. e. cummings
                   (from "Buffalo Bill 's")

Chapter One

DYLAN was doomed. If he made the right move, he might stave off disaster a little while longer, but the end seemed inevitable. There was only one way out: shake the chessboard and holler "Earthquake!" the way Albert the Alligator did in those old Pogo comic strips Dylan's dad loved so much.

Dylan kept looking for a loophole, but it wasn't easy to concentrate. His dad was tapping his fingers on the tray-table, and the guy in the other bed, a crabby auto parts salesman named Groh, was watching some godawful soap opera. Loud. Then a girl in a uniform that looked sort of like a nurse's, but not quite, came in and asked Groh how he was doing.

"Lousy," he barked, waving her aside. "And I'm trying to watch my show."

"Sorry," the girl mumbled, and came over to Dylan's dad's bed.

The girl destroyed Dylan's concentration completely. She was either ugly or beautiful; Dylan couldn't decide which. She had dark frizzy hair and a biggish nose and lips so full and dark that lipstick would have made them almost frightening. Her eyes were even more exceptional. They were big, too, and dark—and more intense than any Dylan had ever seen. "I see you're winning," she told Dylan's father in a throaty voice.

"He sure is," Dylan muttered, glancing back at the board in disgust.

Al Donaldson shrugged. "What can I say? It's absolutely true. Oh, Barbra, this is my son, Dylan."

"Hi," Dylan said, flashing his patented smile, the one that won him friends and women and starring roles in class productions. There was no question at all about whether Dylan was ugly. If they gave college boards for looks and self-confidence, Dylan would have averaged in the 760s. And he knew it.

The smile seemed to bowl Barbra over a little. "Hi," she replied with that slightly sheepish look people get when parents introduce them. She pointed to the chessboard. "You're in big trouble," she informed him.

Dylan nodded glumly. "Any suggestions?"

Barbra studied the board and shook her head. She turned to Al. "How about you? Feeling better?"

"The day I feel better is the day I get out of here," Al snorted.

"That's not supposed to be too much longer, right?"

"Monday, if they're telling me the truth."

"Oh, I'm sure they are," she said in a tone so serious Dylan might have believed it was *her* father who'd just had a bunch of his lymph glands removed. "If I don't get a chance to see you again before you go, good luck."

"Same to you," said Al, extending his hand. "Hey, did you find that old Wardell Gray album?"

"They were out of it. I ordered a copy. Can't wait to hear it."

"You'll love it. The things he did with his sax are absolutely amazing. Simple, but incredible."

She nodded, closing her eyes and purring, as though she were already listening to the music. Then she abruptly broke free of her daydream and told Dylan it was good meeting him.

"Good meeting *you*," Dylan said, turning on the charm. He watched intently as she walked past Groh and out the door. He couldn't tell for sure about her body in that unflattering outfit, but it looked decent at worst. "I resign," he said, standing up.

"Play," his father told him. "She's got the rest of the wing to say hello to. If you want to go talk with her, catch her on her way back."

"What are you, a mind reader?"

"I know that look of yours. Are you saying you're not interested?"

"No. I'm saying I've lost this chess game."

"Well, you're right about that. From this position it'll be mate in eight or nine no matter what you do. One more?"

Dylan grinned. "I don't think we could get it in before she starts back up this way."

"Fine way to treat your poor sick father! Go! And if I don't see you before you head home, tell your mother to send over some salad if it's not too much trouble. The food in here's enough to give a maggot indigestion."

Dylan nodded, sidled past Groh (who scowled at him politely), waved good-bye to Al, and stepped into the hallway. The room hadn't been so terrible, but it always amazed Dylan how depressing a hospital corridor could be. He wondered if it was so gloomy because there was something intrinsically wrong with it, or just because he knew it was in a hospital. If you somehow got plunked down in a hospital corridor and didn't know that's where you were, would it depress you? Probably, he guessed, staring at the endless puke-green walls in the dim fluorescent light and trying to flush the smell of antiseptic from his nostrils.

He turned toward some footsteps. Barbra was walking in his direction. He had hoped she'd have her hands full or need some other kind of help. She looked like a person who wouldn't mind being helped, which was always a good way of getting acquainted. But Barbra was just strolling down the hall, lost in her thoughts. Unpleasant thoughts, Dylan deduced from the look on her face. "Hi," he said.

11

Barbra's gleaming eyes seemed startled to see him. "Did he win?" she asked.

Dylan nodded. "He usually does."

"I know. He beat me in about five minutes the other night."

"Never told me about it," Dylan said with a sly smile. "Sounds like you two have a thing going."

"Oh, come on," she said a little too firmly. "I mean, that's ridiculous. Your father's just a very nice person."

Dylan's smile faded just a little. "If you knew how many times I've heard that."

"Does it bother you? He *is* nice."

"Yeah, he is. Why should it bother me?"

"It shouldn't. You made it sound like it did."

"Not really. He's a good guy. I'm lucky."

"You're *very* lucky."

She said it with such intensity and seriousness that Dylan thought she might actually start to cry. He tried to change the subject. "You have a minute? We could go downstairs for a Coke or something."

"I, uh . . . my break's not till four-thirty."

Dylan glanced at the clock. "That's only ten minutes. I can wait."

"No, listen, maybe I can get it moved up. There isn't a whole lot for me to do today. Sometimes these patients make you feel really useless. They get more out of watching TV than from talking with people."

"Then why do you bother?" Dylan asked as they headed down the hall.

"Somebody has to," she replied in an irritated tone, as though it were a stupid question. "I like to help people. To try, anyway."

They stopped at the nurses' station at the end of the hall. Barbra asked about her break, and the nurse on duty said sure, take your time, no problem, and Dylan and Barbra rode the elevator downstairs. Dylan bought the drinks from a machine. The hospital snack bar was in a corner of the gift shop, and the only clean table was beneath a hanging jungle of stuffed animals. "I keep thinking this giraffe wants me to take him home," Barbra said, reaching up to stroke the toy's plush fur. "Every time I come in here he stares at me with those big dumb eyes of his."

Dylan kept staring into Barbra's big eyes, which were anything but dumb. There was something sad and tender about them, something he had never seen before. "Me," he said, trying to keep things light, "if I were still a kid, I'd probably want that toy car over there or something."

Barbra grinned and shook her head. "Typical Californian."

"What's that supposed to mean?"

"You know: cars, surf, dope. *Fun*," she added, wrinkling her nose.

"You forgot sex," Dylan said. Barbra scowled at him and took a sip of her Coke.

"Well, what's the alternative?" Dylan demanded. "Gloom, dreariness, misery? Besides, last I heard, people were driving cars and smoking grass in North Dakota. No surf, though, I guess."

"Okay, you win," Barbra said. "I was just kidding. I'm not a full-fledged Californian yet. Not even close. Everything's different here from what I'm used to."

"Where you from?"

"New York."

Dylan made a face. "New York *City?*"

"Don't look at me that way. It's not the worst place in the world."

"Not if you're a fan of muggers and murderers and subway slashers."

Barbra's lips tightened into a narrow line. "I'm . . . I'm here now," she stammered, fumbling in her purse for a pack of cigarettes. "Let's not talk about New York. Okay?"

Dylan took the hint. "Okay. Sure. How long have you been out here?"

"Three months," she said, searching anxiously for her matches.

"I've lived here all my life," Dylan told her. "I guess it's hard to adjust when you move around."

"It's hard, all right. Everybody already has their own friends, and you don't know where you fit in. I'll figure it out sooner or later." She lit her cigarette and took a drag on it—something Dylan always found slightly repulsive. She sighed a smoke cloud. "I'll live."

"Ever *try* surfing?" Dylan asked, wishing the smoke would blow the other way.

"You kidding? I'd probably kill myself. I don't even swim very well. You do that, huh? Surfing?"

Dylan shrugged. "A little. I also hang glide."

"Hang glide!"

Dylan smiled. "Typical California kid, right?"

"And you're blond. That counts, too."

"Then are you a typical New York kid? Not that I really have any idea what a typical New York kid would be like. Do you all smoke? We California kids consider that bad for our health."

Barbra's stare bored right through him. "The cigarettes are a crutch, a stupid habit I'm trying to break, okay? Otherwise, I don't think I'm typical anything. I'm interested in old jazz, which is not exactly usual. I play the saxophone a little. I do photography."

"What kind of jazz?"

"Lester Young. Bird. Ellington. Miles. I'm pretty flexible."

"My dad's a big fan."

"Yeah, I know. He caught me humming 'Take the A Train,' and we got talking about it."

"He's got a million jazz records. You should come over and hear some sometime."

Those eyes of hers lit up again. "Is that an invitation?"

14

"Sure."

"Then I'm accepting. Before you change your mind."

"Why should I change my mind?"

Barbra's fingers shook a little as she tapped the ash from her cigarette. "I told you, I don't really fit in here yet. Maybe if you knew me better you'd think I was—what's the word out here—'scazmatic.'"

"Let me decide that, huh? Maybe I would. Or maybe you'll learn something about us 'California kids.'"

Barbra looked at her watch and gulped down the last of her Coke. "I'm going to have to get back," she said. "Listen, I'm really serious about hearing those records." She scribbled something on a paper napkin. "Here's my number. Phone me. And thanks for the Coke."

"Anytime," Dylan said as she stubbed her cigarette out in the cup and got up to leave. Through the jungle of animals he watched her disappear down the hallway.

He looked at the napkin. Barbra Feingold, he said to himself. Barbra Feingold. Wonder why I never noticed her before.

Chapter Two

INSTEAD of paying attention to the movie or to Julie, his sort-of-girlfriend, who was almost in his lap by the time the opening credits were over, Dylan kept thinking about Barbra all evening. Julie was gorgeous, everybody said so, and she obviously adored him, and she was like Silly Putty in his hands, and yet somehow Dylan was beginning to find her . . . well, boring. The only thing she could talk about was gossip—who was going out with who, or who was stoned out of his mind in media class, or who said what to who, or who was pregnant and thinking about getting an abortion. Dylan suddenly found Julie's blond beauty, her flawlessly made-up face, her constantly sunny disposition, almost bland compared to Barbra's dark, exotic mystery. It wasn't just her intense, unusual looks: Barbra seemed different in ways Dylan hadn't even begun to figure out yet.

When he dropped Julie off, he told her he probably couldn't see her the next night, and she pouted coyly and asked why, and he replied that he had something else to do. "Or somebody," Julie said, kissing him on the forehead, but of course she understood, didn't seem the least bit hurt or upset. As usual. When dispositions had been handed out, Julie had been given a double dose of bubbles.

Dylan phoned Barbra the next morning. It might seem a little overeager, but what the hell. He *was* eager.

"Hello?" He recognized the tense, quivery voice. It was her.

17

"It's Dylan. From yesterday at the hospital?"

"Oh," she said nervously. "Hi."

"I thought maybe we could go get something to eat and catch a movie or something tonight."

"What, did your date stand you up?"

"Come on, don't start off a beautiful relationship by being sarcastic. I don't have a date. Do you?"

Dylan listened to a lot of static on the line before she finally answered. "You, if you haven't changed your mind," she said with something like worry in her voice. "I apologize for the sarcasm."

"Okay. How about if I pick you up around, say, five-thirty?"

"Sure. That'd be fine."

"Where do I find you?"

"It's a little complicated. You have a pencil and paper?"

"Hang on a second," he said, leaning across his desk to grab them. "Okay, shoot."

"It's 2232 Sand Arroyo Road. You know where that is?"

"Yeah, more or less. West of the freeway, right?" So that's why he'd never met her before. As he jotted down the directions, he could visualize the drive. Sand Arroyo Road was the winding route up into the most beautiful parts of the hills north of San Felipe. Sand Arroyo Road ran right past the country club. Sand Arroyo Road was up in Meralta, where the rich people lived.

"I think I've got it," he said when she finished. "If I get lost, I'll phone from the eighteenth green."

"Hey, come on. We're not all rich and lazy up here."

"Sorry. Around five-thirty?"

"Right. See you. And thanks for asking."

This was something Dylan hadn't figured on. He didn't know anyone from Meralta. He went to Mission Margarita High, but the kids up there went to

Meralta Hills. The two schools were athletic archrivals. The kids from the hills were all rich and snotty and acted as though they blew their noses with twenty-dollar bills or maybe just snorted coke through rolled-up tens. Or at least so everybody said. But then, Barbra wasn't exactly a native. Anyway, it would be interesting.

He took the phone back into his parents' bedroom and walked downstairs. His mother was grading papers at the dining room table. She looked up at Dylan as he ambled past. "Could I talk to you for a second?"

Dylan shrugged. "Sure."

Kate put down her red pencil and took off her glasses. She looked totally worn out, and Dylan knew it wasn't just from overwork. "Could I ask you a favor?"

Dylan shrugged again. "Depends."

"I don't think you're exactly going to want to hear it."

"What is it?" Dylan asked, though he already had a pretty good idea.

"Look, I think you realize I've been under a lot of pressure with Al in the hospital and everything."

Dylan nodded.

"I'd really appreciate it if you'd cancel that hang gliding session tomorrow."

Dylan sighed. He'd guessed right. He knew it was because Kate loved him and wanted to protect him in her motherly way, but it pissed him off all the same. She was always trying to keep him from doing things she was afraid of. It had happened countless times— when he'd decided to backpack into the woods by himself, when he'd begun surfing, when he'd gotten into hang gliding. And naturally everything had always turned out fine. "It's been set for three weeks now," he reminded her. "I had to cancel the first time because of the winds, and then Gil went on vacation. I really don't want to miss out on this."

"I'm just asking you to put it off a couple of weeks. Until your dad's out of the hospital and up and around again."

"What's the point?"

"The point is I'm really sort of a nervous wreck right now, as you may have noticed. I'm not sleeping well, I'm not feeling well, and the thought of your jumping off a cliff tomorrow for the very first time ever is not exactly helping any."

"I'm not jumping. I'm hang gliding. You know I'm careful. I haven't hurt myself except for a couple of little scrapes since I started flying."

"But you've never done it from a cliff before."

"I've told you fifteen times already. It's the same as down at the beach, only higher up."

His mother stared at him. "What if the glider breaks?"

"What if I get into an accident driving to the supermarket? Gliders don't break. I don't think it's happened in years."

"Could you please do this just for me? You know I'm going to worry about you, and I've got enough worries on my mind right now."

"Mom, I can't give up my life just because Dad's in the hospital. We've talked about this a million times. Your worrying doesn't help you any, and for sure it doesn't help anybody else. If Dad's going to get worse, your worrying isn't going to make him any better. And if I'm going to get hurt hang gliding, your worrying isn't going to keep it from happening."

"It will if my worrying keeps you from going off that cliff."

Dylan shook his head. "It won't."

"Do I have to beg you not to go?"

"Do I have to ask Dad to get you to stop hassling me?" Dylan was sure that would end the argument. Kate knew that Al would tell her to stop being silly and let Dylan do what he'd set his mind on. Al was pretty easygoing about what Dylan did, and Dylan rarely let him down. That was part of the reason why Dylan felt so much closer to him than to Kate.

"Thanks for your concern," she said coldly, putting on her glasses and abruptly flipping another paper to the top of the stack.

I pity the poor kid whose paper gets graded next, Dylan thought as he kissed his mother on the forehead. "I'm going to be okay," he said in his most beguiling tone. "Really." Kate's hard look told him she wasn't convinced.

Well, she'd just have to live with it, he told himself as he strode into the garage, where the brilliant red and yellow sail was folded up in the corner. Dismantled, the glider didn't look like much, but just the colors of the fabric could set Dylan's heart racing.

Just standing there in the garage, he could remember almost every one of his flights across the beach, each one unique, each a special thrill. Just thinking about them, he could relive that shivery feeling he got when he'd reach the edge of the dunes and leap off, that incredible gush of adrenaline that grabbed him in the heart and guts in the last split second as he'd dive into flying position and feel the sail grab the air above him. Then came the euphoria of being out there above the sand, not far above, but far enough to be flying, really and truly flying—concentrating, listening to the wind, steadying the descent, landing. The experience was so intense that Dylan could replay it in his head moment by moment.

He could replay it on the beach for real now, too, ever since his parents had done an amazing thing and bought him this glider for his birthday. It had been his dad's idea. His mother had never been exactly overjoyed about his hang gliding, and when she and Al took him out to the garage for his big surprise, her face turned slightly gloomy at his glee. She brightened up a little only when he promised he wouldn't crack it up for at least a week.

Staring at the sail, Dylan remembered how long it had been since he'd flown. Normally he took the glider to the beach two or three times a week, but ever since he'd scheduled the cliff lesson with Gil, he'd held back from flying, not wanting to take any chances, run any risk of bending the frame or messing up the sail or any of the million other little things that could happen but usually don't except when you can least afford them. He had no intention of letting anything short of a typhoon keep him from going off that cliff tomorrow. He imagined himself up there on the ledge, facing into the wind, connecting the wires, unfurling the sail. The thought made his pulse jump.

Driving up the freeway toward Sand Arroyo Road in the twilight that evening, he was still keyed up. He'd kind of frittered the day away, but tomorrow morning he'd be leaping from the cliff, and in ten minutes he'd be seeing the possibly-beautiful Barbra. Until he got off the freeway, he was brimming with his usual confidence, but when he turned onto Sand Arroyo Road, he felt the confidence turn into lemon Jell-O, and as he climbed into the hills, he felt the Jell-O begin to melt.

This was the Big Leagues, all right. Even in the twilight, you could tell this was no cookie-cutter housing tract like the one he lived in, where somebody obviously had come in with a bulldozer once upon a time, leveled the land, and put up houses identical in every way except for the paint and the decorative shutters. You could see from the way light shone from the interiors that here each house was different, unique, set into the land in a way that made at least some apparent sense. Though not all that much, Dylan remembered with a sardonic grin. During the rainy season, a couple of these houses always managed to slip down the hillsides, and his dad was always bitching about the fires up in these hills.

Relaxing a little, Dylan kept one eye on the house numbers on the left. He nearly overshot the hidden entrance Barbra had warned him about, but he made an expert recovery and climbed the drive to the house. As he crested the hill, he breathed a small sigh of relief. The place wasn't some sort of fairy-tale castle or Dickensian mansion, or even one of those ultramodern free-form jobs you saw now and then in the home section of the Sunday paper. From the outside it looked simple—less cluttered, in fact, than the fake pointed front and pseudo-Greek columns of the "colonial" house he lived in. On the other hand, it seemed too simple, too neat—and somehow terribly lonely.

He rang the doorbell. In the middle of the door he noticed a little circle of light—a peephole of some sort so the person inside could see who was outside. People in Dylan's low-key neighborhood didn't believe in such things. He heard three clicks—locks, he guessed. Then the door opened, revealing an extremely attractive girl in an extremely clingy green knit dress.

"Hi," Barbra said. "Come on in."

Dylan just stood there looking. The dress positively stunned him. He couldn't remember the last time he'd seen a girl his age in a dress like that. The girls where he lived didn't wear them. It wasn't done. You put on your jeans, or in hot weather your shorts, and you were ready to go just about anywhere, except to a wedding or something. Dylan suddenly felt slightly foolish in his T-shirt and faded Levis, as though he'd shown up at a costume party without a costume.

"Hi?" Barbra repeated a bit sheepishly.

"You look"—Dylan's smile broadened as he looked her up and down—"exceptional. A knockout."

A light blush spread across Barbra's face, silently thanking him for the compliment. "Come in a minute."

Dylan followed her. No doubt about it; her body was more than decent. But the inside of the house made him feel slightly uncomfortable. He couldn't put his finger on it at first—nothing looked particularly gaudy or out of place. In fact, it all vaguely reminded him of a phrase he'd heard on TV or somewhere: "elegant simplicity." There wasn't much furniture, and what there was seemed spare, purely functional. The pictures on the walls were somehow cold, uninviting; the coffee table was a huge slab of glass on crystal legs; the plants in the corners were the size of small trees, all trunk and branch. The floors were bare, polished wood; a nubby grayish rug matched the sofa. The place was *too* perfect, *too* tasteful; it brought back the lonely feeling Dylan sensed outside.

Then Barbra dimmed the living room lights and took Dylan's breath away. The room's far wall was entirely glass, looking out over the hills and the ocean and San Felipe far below. It was not the kind of view Dylan ever dreamed of being able to see from someone's living room window. "Incredible," he murmured.

"Want to go out on the balcony?" Barbra asked. "It's even better from out there."

He nodded mechanically. The whole situation was beginning to overwhelm him a little. Barbra's dress, the view, the giant wall of records he noticed in the hallway next to a stereo system of the sort he'd never seen anywhere but the windows of Meralta's fanciest hi-fi shops—it was too much to handle all at once. He followed Barbra to the balcony in a daze.

She was right. The view was even more spectacular from outside. It surrounded you, enveloped you. Way off in the distance, across a couple of low hills, you could see the ocean stretching out, with the thinnest sliver of a moon reflected in it, and down to the south, the electric twinkle of San Felipe, serene in the evening light. It made Dylan wish he could sprout wings—or at least his glider—to sail across it all.

Tentatively, a little bit unsure of herself, Barbra pointed out the sights. She thought the rise to the right was Mount San Manuel, but she always got it confused with Mount San Felipe, which was closer, unless she had it backwards. If the cove straight ahead had an official name, she'd forgotten it, but somebody had told her it was one of the best spots for surf fishing. As she pointed toward San Felipe Bay, Barbra stared at Dylan as though she desperately wanted him to approve of all this. Catching the spice of her perfume in the cool night air, Dylan approved more than he dared let her know.

"I never realized how beautiful it was up here," he said.

Barbra sighed as she led him back into the house and down a long hallway. "It *is* quite a place. I've counted something like twenty-three different species of birds at our feeder without even trying. But what really impresses me about this house is the garage. After you've lived in a New York apartment all your life, you kind of get used to not having anywhere you can work on something really messy. I've got a darkroom out there now, and it's wonderful. I'd show you, but . . . well, it's kind of filthy."

They walked through a doorway. "My room." It, too, had the magical view. It, too, seemed spare, almost empty, with a mattress on the floor and a white desk in one corner and a music stand in the other. But on one wall hung three saxophones in increasing sizes, and over the bed were posters of three black musicians Dylan didn't recognize. Dylan didn't quite know how to react.

"Scazmatic, huh?" Barbra asked disappointedly.

"Different," Dylan offered. He gestured toward the saxophones. "You play all three of those?"

"Not all at once."

"I hope not."

"Rahsaan Roland Kirk could. Me, I'm lucky when they sound okay one at a time."

"Let's hear."

"Oh, come on . . ."

"Play something for me."

Barbra shook her head nervously.

"Really," Dylan said, turning on that million-dollar charm. "I'd like to hear you."

"You sure?"

Dylan nodded and smiled another million. Shaking her head, Barbra wrestled the middle sax down from the wall, moistened the reed, and put her fingers on the keys. She took a deep breath. Then the music came out.

It was warm, sensual, romantic—and slightly familiar, something Dylan dimly remembered hearing on one of his father's records. As she neared the end of the melody, those dark, liquid eyes of hers asked him if he wanted her to go on, and he nodded, and she kept the sound flowing without missing a beat. It was wonderful, dream music that conjured up whole worlds of shadow and musk. "Beautiful," he said honestly when she finished. "Really beautiful."

"It ought to be," she said, shaking the spit from the sax. "'Body and Soul,' Coleman Hawkins version. I spent about three months figuring out how to swipe his phrasing. Even so, it's just a poor imitation."

As she hung the sax back on the wall, Dylan stood there admiring her. She looked spectacular. She wasn't exactly the girl of his dreams; she was so far outside his experience that he could never have dreamed of anyone like her. His plans for a quick run to Burger King and the Mall Cinema afterward would need some changing. The King of Burgers wasn't anywhere near royal enough for someone like Barbra. But Dylan wasn't dressed for a fancy place, and he couldn't have afforded one anyhow.

Brainstorm. "How do you feel about Mexican food?" he asked.

Barbra grabbed the sax, played a few bars of "La Cucaracha," and shouted "Olé!"

* * *

The restaurant's booths were enclosed in tall wooden panels with bright Mexican colors at the top. It was like sharing a little room together. Except when the waiter or busboy came by, Dylan and Barbra were totally alone. The rest of the planet might not have existed.

Her father couldn't eat Mexican food—ulcer trouble, Barbra said—so she had to sneak out to taco stands and burrito joints when she got the chance. Which wasn't often, since she didn't drive.

Dylan couldn't believe it. It was impossible to grow up without learning to drive. You might as well be crippled. But in New York, Barbra explained, you could take buses everywhere. Or cabs, which were kind of expensive until you figured out how much it cost a person to keep a car in the city in terms of parking and insurance and fenders and trouble, at which point cabs began to seem like a bargain.

"What about the famous New York subways?" Dylan asked.

The muscles of Barbra's face suddenly went slack.

"That bad, huh?" Dylan said, dipping a tortilla chip into the hot sauce.

Her eyes misted over. "Uh, let's not talk about it, okay?"

Dylan nodded as she dug into her purse for a cigarette. It was a new experience for him, the way she

27

reacted when it came to certain questions about her old home town. He'd known people to change the subject good-naturedly when the conversation veered too close to their sore points, but he'd never seen anyone get so serious about it. "Are you at least learning to drive?" he asked, hoping to steer the talk in a more pleasant direction.

"Yeah," she said, lighting up. "I'm taking driver's ed at school. Everybody thinks it's strange. I'm the oldest kid in my class."

The nachos arrived. Barbra went absolutely apeshit over the fiery jalapeño peppers on top. And she adored the chiles rellenos. She said they vaguely resembled a soufflé she used to love at this insanely expensive French restaurant in New York, only they were probably better. It made Dylan very glad he'd remembered this place.

They began discussing other differences between California and New York. To Barbra, everybody in the West seemed so—she wasn't sure of the right word; *mellow* and *laid back* didn't exactly cover it—easygoing compared with the hostility of people back East.

"Maybe people just let it out more there," Dylan suggested.

"Maybe. But I think they really *are* more hostile. Back there you see people fighting in the street or swearing at each other for half an hour over a parking space. It makes your own hostility start flowing. Here, everything kind of fades into the scenery."

Dylan shrugged. He'd never really thought about it.

"Or maybe it's just me," she went on, staring sullenly at her plate. "I sort of stick out from the scenery. I'm not cool enough. I'm not athletic enough. I'm not blond enough."

Dylan reached across the table and touched her hand. "You're perfect," he told her.

He could tell she knew it wasn't just a line. The sudden sparkle in her eyes cut through her seriousness like a flashlight in a forest. Then she nervously stubbed out her cigarette in an ashtray with a cactus painted on it.

They skipped the movie. Dylan drove Barbra down to his favorite cove, and they huddled close in the Blazer and listened to the waves lap in on the shore. He had been there, often, with other girls, but never before had he felt so—well, romantic had to be the word for it. Pounding away so hard he could almost hear it thump, his heart seemed to have swollen to twice its normal size.

They talked quietly about how beautiful this place was, and then Barbra said they'd probably better be getting back, and Dylan leaned over and kissed her, and even though she had that unmistakable taste of stale cigarette smoke they kept on kissing for a very long time, and finally Barbra gave him a special look, her eyes saying, unless he misread them, that she didn't want to stop but felt she had to, and her lips saying plainly that she'd had a wonderful evening, really, and although sex was not the furthest thing from Dylan's mind, he sensed it would be entirely out of place to suggest it right now.

He drove her home and they kissed good night. When she left, it only worsened the thumping in his chest and the weakness in his legs and the fogginess in his head that he suspected he would have to blame on love.

Chapter Three

THOSE lips and eyes of hers kept haunting Dylan all night long. When the alarm went off at six the next morning, he seriously considered phoning and inviting her to come watch him fly. But it was totally crazy to even think about waking somebody up at that hour on a Sunday, and knowing she was there was not going to make his flying any easier. Better to keep his mind on the job. He'd have plenty of time to show off once he got good at this.

He got up, washed, dressed, gulped some orange juice, and went into the garage. He loaded the glider into the Blazer, tossed the parts kit into the front seat, backed the truck down the driveway, and set off up the street. According to the plan, his friend Crazy Jay was supposed to be waiting in front of his house with Sean and Yolanda, the video wizards of Mission Margarita High. Dylan hoped everybody had managed to wake up, especially Jay. Jay's dad was notorious for his tantrums, especially when he'd been drinking, and Dylan didn't relish the idea of going up to ring the doorbell at six-thirty in the morning.

Jay was waiting, all right, but alone except for his infamous porkpie hat. Jay was probably the only person in San Felipe who insisted on wearing a hat everywhere he went. "Little S and big Y can't make it," he announced wearily as he slumped into the Blazer. "Can't bring themselves to get out of bed this early. Also the camera is out of sync or some damned thing. They phoned late last night and said they'd try to get up to the ledge sometime before ten or so."

"By ten or so the flying may be over."

"You know the terrible twosome," Jay said with a shrug. "Besides, I'm the number one stunt driver around here. I'll find you wherever you come down."

"Yeah," Dylan said. "That's what I'm afraid of."

"Look, I told you, that thing with my pickup was a pure accident. The tree stepped out of nowhere and sideswiped me, was all. There's absolutely no way to defend yourself against stupid trees."

"I'd still feel better if Sean were along to slow you down a little."

"He'd slow us down plenty. Sounded like he and Yolanda had another hot night. Probably what's wrong with the camera is they burned it out taking pictures. How was the rich girl?"

Dylan scowled. "Who said she was rich? And where'd you hear about that, anyway?"

"Answer B: word gets around. Answer A: if she lives up in Meralta, she's rich, all right. How was she?"

Dylan shrugged. "She's okay."

"How okay?"

"Come on, lay off."

"Is she?"

"Is she what?"

"Rich."

"I didn't ask for her financial statement."

"Okay, you don't have to get weird. I just asked." Jay slouched down in the seat and put his hat over his face as if to nap.

"Hope Gil didn't oversleep," Dylan muttered.

Jay pushed his hat back a little. "From what you say, that guy's so dependable, it's sickening. Hey, I've almost got my old man convinced."

"Convinced what?"

"To pay for gliding lessons. Then you won't be the only one out there having fun. You do realize this morning I could be down at the beach with some beautiful lady."

"More like trying to pick up somebody else's lady."

"I'd just like a little recognition for my noble sacrifice."

"Christ, it's not as though I tied you up and dragged you here."

"Man, you are really sensitive today. Itchy, you know?"

Dylan knew, all right. It was a whole combination of things: his father's illness, his mother's worries, his feelings about the "rich" girl, the fact that in half an hour he'd be sailing out over a thousand-foot drop. Things like that had a way of making you sensitive. Itchy.

He drove through the flatlands, then wound up the road into the mountains. Dylan knew the roads well; he'd been up there on the ledges any number of times, watching Gil and other expert gliders practice and compete. In a few minutes it'd be his turn.

"You scared?" Jay inquired.

"Sure. A little." Dylan hoped it was just a little.

"Me, I'd be petrified."

"It's not supposed to be all that different from the dunes."

"Just about a thousand feet higher, is all."

"Something like that."

"Guess you'll find out."

"Guess so."

Dylan recognized Gil's pickup on the dirt clearing at the back of the ledge and spotted Gil's massive body and red beard near the edge. Gil was looking down, holding his hand out, feeling the way the wind came up from the drop. Dylan turned off the engine and jumped out of the Blazer.

"Terrible day," Gil said matter-of-factly as he strolled over. "Can't let you go out there."

Dylan felt his stomach desert him. "You've got to be kidding."

The corners of Gil's eyes crinkled up. "Yeah. Conditions are just about perfect."

Dylan exhaled a sigh of relief. This wasn't something he could wait for any longer.

"Get yourself set up," Gil said. "Your friend may as well head down to the landing site and set up the streamers." He turned toward Jay. "Know where it is?"

"I know where it's supposed to be."

"Well, nobody moved it, unless there was an earthquake I didn't hear about. So get on down there, because your man is going to come in about three inches away from your nose."

"Glad to hear you have such confidence in me," Dylan said, lugging the glider out of the Blazer.

"You'd damn well better come in on target," Gil told him. "How am I ever going to sign this dude up for lessons if you make me look bad?"

Jay got into the Blazer. "Good luck, Flash!" he shouted as he started it up. "See you downstairs!" He took off in a cloud of dust that made Dylan wonder if the truck would still be in one piece by the end of the day.

Gil put one hand on the glider. "I want you to check the wind before you set up. Go ahead over. I'll hang onto this thing till you get back."

Dylan went to the edge and looked down. The whole valley was spread out before him in the sharp morning light. He spotted the cleared-out landing area in the middle of the brush down below. He felt the wind whoosh over the edge. Gil hadn't been lying about those perfect conditions.

"You feel it? You got the picture?" Gil hollered.

Dylan nodded. He went back, took the glider from Gil's hands, and carried it closer to the edge. Standing the frame into the wind, he began the setup procedures Gil had made him memorize and repeat and recite so many times that by now they were probably implanted in his genes.

Carefully, methodically, he connected the stranded

34

flying wires to the bright aluminum keel. Next he fastened the keel wire and the long metal king post together. He spread the crossbar, and then the leading edges of the sail, which blossomed into a heart-stopping billow of scarlet and gold. There were the side wires to take care of, and a double check to make sure all the vital connectors were fastened properly. Then—Dylan felt the adrenaline pumping now, but he didn't let it interfere with his concentration—he tightened the turnbuckles just enough to take up the slack in the wires. If he'd done everything right, the glider was ready to fly.

He made the final checks and put on his helmet. He strapped on his harness and attached it to the glider. There was nothing left to do but make one last inspection. Dylan examined the nuts and bolts, looked over all the cables, made sure all the safety pins were in place. "Ready!" he hollered to Gil.

Gil inspected the rig more thoroughly than usual, and usually he didn't overlook a thing. He pressed on the wires, nudged the bolts, and tugged at the straps, grunting a little when each item met with his approval. He stepped away for an overall look at the whole rig. Then he came back and put his arm on Dylan's shoulder.

"Looks okay," he said, putting his face right next to Dylan's. "Tell me what you're going to do."

When Gil's steel blue eyes bored into you, you knew you'd better get things right the first time. "I'm going to head for the edge, jump off, and take command with the control bar, as usual. Then I'll go for the landing area, watch the streamers, and land into the wind."

"What don't you do?"

"Crack up."

Gil frowned. "Seriously."

"I don't come up above the level of the cliff."

"Right. You also don't go looking for thermals, you

35

don't go trying for an extra-long ride, you don't forget to listen to that wind in your sail, and you don't start thinking about anything else but the fact that you're one hell of a long way up and you want to get down in one piece. First do the job. Save the fancy stuff for later. Got it?"

Dylan nodded. "Okay," Gil said, squeezing his shoulder. "Keep track of that wind, and you're on your own." Gil patted him on the back and went to the edge to watch.

Dylan lifted the glider into takeoff position and looked up at the fluttering sail. He tugged on his harness one last time. He sucked in his breath, took a final glance at Gil, and froze.

His heart was pounding like a jackhammer now. The only way to silence it would be to get going. He ran to the edge and jumped.

For an instant he felt a ripple of sheer terror as he leaned forward on the control bar in midair. Then he felt the sail do its work. He was flying. He was in control. The ground was hundreds of feet below. It was awesome.

Concentrate, concentrate, he kept telling himself, since it was easy to get carried away—literally carried away—at a time like this. Blue and red and yellow above, green and brown below, Dylan in between —it was better than he had imagined, the way he was floating, drifting downward in total silence except for the wind whooshing past his ears.

Concentrate, concentrate. He spotted the landing area. Jay was looking up, his hand shading his eyes against the sun. The fabric streamers he'd set up showed how the wind was blowing down there. The streamers still looked tiny, but that was when you had to plan your landing. By the time they got big, it'd be too late to make changes.

A little gust sent Dylan off to the right, and he shifted his weight over the bar to compensate. The ground wind, he could see from the streamers, was blowing in at a slightly different angle from the air aloft. He moved a little farther out to allow for it.

The ground was coming up fast now, brushy stuff you would not want to land in (and neither would the glider). The clearing was just ahead. Dylan slowed his descent, skimmed the ground, put the glider into a stall, and gently touched down.

"Fantastic!" Jay yelled, waving his hat wildly as he rushed over. "Fan-damn-tastic!"

Dylan didn't yell back. He wanted to be professional about this, tend to the glider, take care of the usual postflight chores. But his inner voice was deafening. In amazed satisfaction, it was shouting "Terrific!" and "Wow!" and "You did it!" He had made that trip a hundred times in his imagination, but those flights of fancy were just jokes compared with the real thing. "Goddamn!" he whooped.

He couldn't wait to sail again. He hardly noticed Jay's lousy driving as they headed back to the ledge. Again and again he sailed down the hill, and each time Gil gave him pointers to improve his technique. By the end of the session, he felt confident, experienced—and so exhilarated he couldn't begin to express it.

As he dismantled his glider for the day, the experts began their flights up above. The sky filled with sails as the best of the fliers picked out thermals and magically rose in those columns of warm air. Dylan had watched them often, but today he skipped it and went out celebrating with Jay. He knew he'd soon be catching those thermals himself.

Chapter Four

"AT HOSPITAL. Phone me," read the note in his mother's handwriting that was waiting for him on the refrigerator when he got home. Dylan already knew the hospital number without having to look it up, and he grabbed an apple out of the fridge while the receptionist put him through to his father's room. It was Al who answered.

"Hi," Dylan said. "What's up?"

"How was the great leap forward?" his father asked.

"Incredible. You can't believe."

"No? I still remember the first time I had to jump from the fifth story of the rescue-training tower. Wait a minute; your mother is looking at me as if to ask whether you're okay."

Dylan scowled. "Of course I'm okay. I'm terrific."

There was a long silence at the other end of the line. Then a stifled voice that Dylan barely recognized as Al's said, "Well, pal, that makes one of us."

"Huh?"

"Why don't you come on over here and we'll talk about it?" Al said in a flat tone. "I want to hear all about this flying of yours anyhow."

"Are you all right?" Dylan asked, his throat suddenly dry from worry.

"Got any previous engagements?"

"No, I just want to know if you're . . ."

"Look, get on over," his father interrupted. "We'll talk about it then."

The line went dead. Dylan had planned on showering, but now he sensed an air of—well, not quite emergency, but close. That strange flatness in his father's voice—what could possibly be causing it? Dylan changed clothes in a hurry and headed for the hospital wondering what in hell could be troubling his father any more than the troubles he'd gone through already.

Toward the end of Dylan's junior year, his father had gone in for a physical, and the doctor had noticed a little growth of some sort on his back. No big deal, the doctor said, just have a dermatologist take it off. Dylan's dad didn't care much for doctors, didn't take the advice, and forgot the whole thing. Six months later Dylan's mother noticed the wart or mole or whatever it was one night. She claimed it had gotten bigger. Al didn't think so, but Kate put up such a fuss that he finally went to see the dermatologist. No big deal, the dermatologist said, and took the growth off. Three days later the biopsy came back. The growth was a melanoma—a cancer. And the cancer had spread.

To anybody else it would have been a terrible blow. Anybody else would have pissed and moaned about how unfair life was. Not Al Donaldson. Dylan's father was the bravest person he had ever known. He had the medals to prove it: Maltese crosses festooned with ribbons, ribbons without the crosses, and page after page of fancy-script citations, honors, and awards for meritorious service, valor, courage. Al was a fireman, and not just any fireman. The boys (and two women) at the firehouse would tell Dylan every chance they got: Al Donaldson was the best.

Apparently he had no fear of death. "We all have to die sometime," he'd say calmly at the dinner table after risking his neck to rescue grandfathers, mothers, babies, and even cats from burning buildings where other firefighters had died. As far as he was concerned, his cancer was a lot like a fire. It was something that had to be extinguished, something he would handle, and that would be that.

Dylan tried to take it exactly the same way. If Al wasn't going to let this get him down, then neither was he. When Al went into the hospital, Dylan visited him every chance he could. The cancer had spread to some lymph nodes, and they had to be removed. It wasn't the most horrible operation in the world, as Al kept telling everybody, but it did tear you up for a while, and the incisions weren't things you could just ignore and go out and fight fires with the next day. Al was as brave as ever about it, laughing and joking the moment the anesthetic wore off. Dylan knew he'd come out on top, as usual. It was just something that had to be lived through.

As he parked the car in the hospital lot, Dylan was still trying to guess what might be on his father's mind. Al was supposed to come home from the hospital the next day; maybe they'd decided to make him stay another week. Or maybe his father's strange tone was a joke or something, a sneaky way of getting him over to the hospital for some sort of surprise celebration for his hang gliding. It would be just like Al to pull that kind of thing.

As usual, the gloomy hospital corridors did their best to dampen Dylan's spirits. He wondered how in hell anybody ever managed to get well in the midst of all this ugliness. Then he turned in to his father's room.

Groh had disappeared. Dylan's parents were alone there. They had the look of people who'd been crying and were making an extreme effort to tough it out. The scene didn't look anything like a surprise party.

"Hi," said Al, obviously trying hard to sound normal.

"What's going on?" Dylan asked cautiously.

"Tell us about your day," Al replied.

"Later," Dylan said. "You tell me about yours."

Al looked at Kate for support. She bit her lip and cocked her head to one side without saying a word. "Sit down," Al told his son. Dylan kept standing.

"Suit yourself," Al said, sighing and nervously pressing his fingertips together. "We heard from the doctor. I'm still going home tomorrow. As scheduled."

"Great!" said Dylan.

His father exhaled. "Not exactly. It turns out they didn't get all the cancer."

"You mean they're going to have to operate again?"

Al hesitated, had trouble finding the right words. When they came, they came all at once, as if they were some vile poison he needed to spit out. "They can't operate. Damned stuff is in my liver."

Dylan sat down, stunned. "Shit," he muttered.

Al nodded. "That's what I said, too. It's a pretty accurate description. They tell me I have maybe six months left. At most."

Dylan felt as if he were being strangled from inside. He knew if he tried saying anything, it would get stuck somewhere way down in his throat. He didn't know what to say anyway. "Can't they do anything?" he finally blurted out.

Al shrugged. "That's cancer. Most types they can do something about. Some types they can't. This is one of the can'ts."

"What are you supposed to do?"

His father shook his head slowly. "Nothing else *to* do. Take it. Live with it. Go home and let the incisions heal. Come in for radiation treatments and maybe chemotherapy to slow the thing down a little. Enjoy the time I have left the best I can."

"I still think we ought to get another opinion," Kate said.

"Sure," Al agreed. "Fine. But let's not kid ourselves. Unless we find somebody who's a lot more optimistic than the guy who's been treating me—and he's supposed to be damned good—I'm going to be gone before the end of the year. Probably sooner. At least we'll have time to make some plans."

Suddenly, uncontrollably, Dylan found tears rolling down his cheeks. Dull pain throbbed inside his head, an overwhelming pain that seemed impossible to drive away. What was bringing the pain wasn't the thought of his father dying, because Dylan could barely even imagine that. What was making him cry was the beauty of the way his father was standing up under it, that unshakable bravery Al had won all those medals for.

"I know," Al told him gently, hesitantly. "It's going to be rough on you and Kate. I mean, I've seen what's happened when guys in the firehouse have gotten killed. It's going to be a lot harder on you than it is on me. At least afterward. I don't know how I'd handle it myself if I were you."

Bravely, Dylan knew. Bravely. But bravery was Al's way. Dylan didn't know what his own way was. In a sense his father's sympathy was only making things harder. Right then, Dylan felt what he needed was something to strike back at, something to relieve the rage and anger and frustration he felt toward a world so mercilessly cruel as to take heroes like Al away at a ridiculously early age while letting the villains go on forever. But there was nothing to lash out against except fate, and fate wasn't right there in front of him. Sniffling, Dylan tried to pull himself together.

"Look, we'll have plenty of time to talk all this out," Al said quietly. "Tell me about the gliding."

Silence filled the room like the smell of antiseptic. The last thing Dylan wanted to talk about now was flying. His own confrontation with fate, with danger, with death, had suddenly become trivial, since it turned out that death didn't actually fly up and meet you in the sky but instead sneaked through your blood and caught you in an ugly hospital room.

But Dylan knew Al really wanted to hear about his gliding, so he stifled his rage and tried his best to communicate the glorious birdlike feeling he got from controlling his path through the soundless, invisible billows of air. Al made Dylan go into every detail, even joked that he'd have to take up gliding himself once he got back home. Then he announced that he was a little tired and wanted to take a nap, which was a not-so-subtle hint that he wanted to be left alone for a while. Kate leaned over the bed and kissed him, and Dylan squeezed his hand and hugged him, and then Dylan and his mother went out into corridors that looked even uglier than ever.

They didn't say a word until they got out of the building, as though somehow the poisonous walls might overhear. Kate's face was a display window for her thoughts. She was drained, all cried out. She finally spoke when they reached the parking lot. "How do you feel?" she asked.

Dylan wasn't quite sure he could put it into words. He wasn't even sure how he felt. "How do *you* feel?"

"Angry," she said bitterly. "Frustrated, incredibly frustrated. You never imagine something like this could happen. Everybody keeps telling you things are going to work out fine."

Dylan didn't know what to say. He still felt as though he'd been kicked in the guts.

"I'll take the Blazer," his mother told him. "I want to go off somewhere and be alone for a while."

Dylan nodded and tried to keep himself together as she drove off in the brilliant sunlight that seemed to be mocking their sadness. Then he kicked the Honda's left front tire, slammed his fist down on the hood, and, when that failed to ease his pain, got inside and wept until his eyes burned.

Chapter Five

NEXT evening they held a private homecoming party for Al. There was Kate's famous lasagna. There was an enormous salad with Al's celebrated dressing as interpreted by co-chef Dylan. There was a Cabernet Sauvignon they'd been saving for a really special occasion. There was a homemade superchocolate welcome-home cake. There was a sense of good feeling at being back together again. And there was an extra guest at the table: death.

Well, not physically at the table in his grim reaper suit, picking his fingernails with his scythe, but hovering in the air somehow, a presence as gloomy as that black cloak of his. Yet maybe death wasn't there at all. That was what struck Dylan as so weird about the situation. Here they were pigging out, getting drunk, cracking jokes, while his father was dying. But was he? Maybe it had all been some gruesome mistake, a switch of the hospital records or something. Stuff like that probably happened all the time.

Al certainly wasn't playing the part of a dying man very well. From the minute he got home, he was like a caged panther, a dynamo of pent-up energy, itching to get back to the firehouse the instant his incisions healed. For the first couple of days he was satisfied to take it easy, read or play games with Kate or Dylan, but then he began to stalk through the house looking for something to *do*, damn it. He cleaned the windows, he polished the silver, and one afternoon Dylan found him in the garage waxing the family bicycles, for godsake. Anything to keep his hands busy. Kate warned him to slow down, not to do something foolish that might somehow open his incisions, but in fact he was healing quickly and well from the operation—which in itself convinced her that the doctors' diagnosis might have been wrong. Al, always the realist, told her not to get her hopes up.

Neither Dylan nor Kate could find the strength to discuss death with Al, so they pointedly avoided the subject. When his father won at chess, Dylan would carefully remind himself not to say, "You killed me" or "You slaughtered me," though he realized his deliberate silences spoke louder than words. His mind was on tiptoe.

Yet he knew he had to face up to it: death was no longer something that happened to somebody somewhere someday, something that happened to people you hardly knew. Death was real, and it was coming into his life.

Of course, it had been part of his life all along. He'd just chosen to ignore it. He couldn't remember how many of his father's friends and co-workers had died fighting fires over the years, but he could remember all too clearly the day he learned that his favorite grandparents, his mother's parents, had been killed in a car crash. He had cried, he had grieved, he had gotten over it, but now death seemed to surround him. The news was death: wars, murders, terrorists, bombings, riots, kidnapping, accidents. TV and movies were death—car chases and shootouts. Books were death. Death was everywhere, a cold unignorable fact.

But a slippery one. Aside from the fact that he had to die sometime, Al's impending doom was really only a matter of opinion, an educated guess. Some doctors said it would happen. The same doctors had been talking about a cure, or at least a recovery, only a few days earlier. Why believe them now when they were so wrong before? And yet how could you not believe them?

What was he supposed to tell his friends? His parents agreed there was nothing to be ashamed of, nothing to hide. But when Dylan told Jay, all Jay could say was, "Rough, man. At least it's not your fault." Not much comfort.

Of course it wasn't his fault. Or was it? Those two words, "of course," were becoming a lot less meaningful every day. A while ago his father's cancer wasn't serious, "of course." He'd recover quickly, "of course." Of course. Maybe it *was* Dylan's fault somehow.

And the whole damned thing had come up at such a terrible time—of course! Not that there was a particularly good time for a father you loved to die on you. But it was Dylan's senior year, and school had finally begun to release its iron grip. Dylan was caught up in the excitement—and apprehension—of knowing he'd be making a clean break with that part of his past in the fall instead of returning to the places and faces that had been so familiar for so long. His college boards had turned out better than he'd expected. A couple of his classes were actually interesting. He'd won the starring role in the media class's senior film. He'd had that first taste of high-level hang gliding. And now there was Barbra.

But how were you supposed to go through the motions, live your life as if nothing special were happening, when your father was dying right before your eyes? It would have been the best time of his life, Dylan thought bitterly, but this thing with Al was poisoning everything.

Especially Dylan's attitude. The next time he saw Barbra, he was not in the best of moods. For the first time since coming home, Al had had a bad day, spending most of his time in bed, too weak to do much more than turn on the radio. Kate had hassled

Dylan about doing the shopping, which wouldn't've been so terrible if he hadn't gotten in line behind some angry-looking middle-aged lady who insisted the clerk had made a mistake and made him check every single item on the $142.64 register tape. Then the clerk had run out of tape, and Dylan had to stand there helplessly while somebody went to find some. On the way to Barbra's he had to suffer through a hellish freeway traffic jam caused by people gawking at the remains of a two-car accident so bloody he couldn't bear to glance at it.

By the time he got to Barbra's door, he was seething with frustration. She led him in, told him to sit down for a minute or two, she was running late.

"That figures," Dylan snapped.

"I'm sorry. I was practicing and I lost track of the time."

"Everybody's losing track of everything," Dylan grumbled.

Barbra stared at him in exasperation. "Do you get this way on a regular basis? I mean, I thought Californians were supposed to be mellow."

"I wish you'd lay off that 'typical Californian' crap."

"Listen, maybe we should call this off. It's not exactly starting out to be a pleasant evening."

Dylan exhaled. "Look, I'm sorry. I really want to be with you tonight."

"Me, too. I just wish you'd calm down a little. Come on," she said. "You can sit in the bathroom and we can talk through the door while I get dressed."

"I'd rather watch."

"I'll bet you would." She led the way down the hall and changed the subject. "How was your flight? Or don't you call it that? I mean, that's what I'd ask somebody who just got back from the East Coast."

Dylan shrugged. "Incredible," he said in a flat tone.

"Really sounds it," she said sarcastically.

He tried to make it more convincing. "Really. It was."

"You don't seem exactly excited about it."

"Look, Barbra, I've had a hellish week. I can't feel today the way I felt when I did it."

"What happened?"

Dylan hesitated, unsure of how much he should say. He wondered if the whole thing with his father wasn't something just too private to bring her into. After all, he hardly knew her. But she'd met Al, and telling her about him might get him some sympathy, and sympathy was something he needed very badly right then. "My father's dying," he said quietly.

Barbra turned and stared at him. "That's terrible," she said in a choked voice. Her face went limp, and her eyes filled with deep tear pools. She was too damned sensitive, Dylan told himself. He wished he'd kept his mouth shut. He could hardly bear it when she finally forced words out in a stifled whisper: "Listen, I know what you're going through."

"How could you?" he said bitterly. "How could you?"

Her next words came out automatically, weakly, as if she had said them so many times she was weary of them: "My mother was murdered."

For a moment Dylan stood there stupefied as tears rolled down Barbra's cheeks. Then he held her close as she cried.

She never did change her clothes, and they never did get to the movies that night. Instead, they drove down the hill to a quiet little place Barbra had discovered and shared a pizza. And their stories.

Barbra's mother had been stabbed to death in a robbery in a New York subway station. It was the kind of thing that happened all the time, Barbra said, puffing nervously on her cigarette: senseless, random violence that everybody ignores. Until it happens to them. Afterwards, her father put in for a transfer from the New York office, and that's how they happened to come west. Her father lost himself in work and drink; the only way she could get him to come out of his grief and keep him halfway sober was by insisting he drive her places, which was one reason she hadn't rushed to get her driver's license. But she hadn't gotten over the pain any more than he had.

She still kept reliving the night of her mother's death. She still kept remembering how she'd waited for her mother to come home from her office uptown at Columbia University, and how it had gotten later and later, and how her mother didn't answer her office phone, and how around eleven o'clock there was a phone call for her father, who was out of town, and how she knew—just sensed somehow, but *knew*— that something horrible had happened.

Even before the murder, her father had been a real workaholic, away on business a lot, and Barbra and her mother had grown close, leaning on each other for all sorts of support. It was her mother who'd gotten her interested in art and books and music; they'd shared all kinds of beautiful experiences, and then suddenly, unbelievably, her mother was gone. Even now, almost a year after the killing, the one thing Barbra could not shake off was the feeling she was somehow responsible for her mother's death. Even though she knew she couldn't be.

Dylan nodded somberly. "I feel the same way about my father and this cancer."

Barbra reached across the table and touched his hand. "It hurts, Dylan. It hurts a lot. At least you have time. You can prepare for it."

"I don't know if that's good or bad. It hurts already."

"Maybe you're right. Maybe it's better just to go along as if everything is normal and then have to deal with the one big shock."

Dylan shrugged. "Who knows? You don't get to choose. What happens, happens, and you're stuck with it."

They drove to the beach again and watched the little waves lap in. As they talked about their lives, Dylan felt he had never been so close to another human being. It was almost as though he could see her thoughts inside her head, and he wondered if his emotions were as obvious to her. In a way it was almost frightening, but it was also comforting in a way he desperately needed. At least he wasn't alone. At least there was one other person in the world who had some idea what he was going through. Dylan had never felt so sad and so happy at the same time.

Chapter Six

A COUPLE of days later, the second specialist confirmed the first one's opinion. There had been no mistake. Al was dying, all right. Three to six months seemed a reasonable prediction. The girl would send a bill—fast, Al guessed sardonically, considering the prognosis.

That was Al's way. A little joke to lighten the gloom. And confronting the issue head on—that was also his way. In one of his peppier moments he'd gone to the library and ransacked the shelves for every book on death he could find. When Dylan saw the pile on the coffee table, he protested that it couldn't be precisely what Al needed to cheer him up, and prescribed a dose of Mark Twain or Brautigan or somebody as an antidote. But Al never took the advice. The guys at the firehouse had nicknamed him "Plato" for his habit of reading philosophy and literature instead of *Playboy*, and every time Dylan went into the living room he'd find his father in the recliner with his nose buried in some ghastly volume about dying. Sometimes Al would be snoring; he was slowly growing weaker, and often he would spend whole afternoons or evenings asleep.

Dylan tried the best he could not to let it get him down. He worked on his hang gliding, he immersed himself in chemistry homework, he learned his lines for the film. Sweet bubbly Julie was his leading lady, which had once delighted him but now began to get on his nerves. She had the habit of phoning or dropping by at odd hours to ask how she should read such-and-such a line, or whether she should play scene twelve facing him or looking the other way. "Yolanda's the director," Dylan would reply. "Ask her." But Julie kept insisting that it was his opinion that she really valued.

Her unbelievably unsubtle attempts at winning him back finally wore him down. He blurted out that he was seeing someone else, that he didn't want to see her anymore. That solved absolutely nothing. Julie said he'd change his mind; besides, she didn't mind sharing.

"It's the price of stardom," Jay told him one morning on the way to the cliff. "It's a nuisance you'll have to live with, but believe me, Julie's one nuisance I wouldn't mind living with. I'd take her off your hands myself, but unfortunately, she only goes for bareheaded guys who happen to be gorgeous."

The hatless Adonis began running up to Meralta every chance he got. He loved hanging out with Barbra, roaming through the hills or meandering along the beaches to the accompaniment of her New York accent, seeing his California world with her New York eyes, and then entering a new world that was hers—visiting her darkroom, listening to her records, driving up into the mountains and playing in the snow. He'd guessed right about her name: she was indeed named after Streisand, who—no kidding! —had been a friend of her mother's way back in grade school. But he was astounded when, unlike everybody he'd ever known, she guessed right about his name: it didn't come from the singer, but from the singer's namesake, Dylan Thomas, the Welsh poet. A poet who—somehow Dylan couldn't avoid bringing it up—died young.

"Nobody ever said love was easy," Jay told him one day when he complained about all the time he was spending en route between San Felipe and Meralta. He was seeing a lot less of his friends, he was working a lot less on his homework, and he was beginning to pay for it by losing sleep. But in spite of all that, despite a continent's worth of differences, despite Barbra's skittishness about sex, the bond between them somehow ran far deeper than the mere coincidence about their parents' early deaths. Barbra helped keep him sane, helped give him strength.

He needed it. Al was beginning to walk around under a dark cloud. More than once, Dylan asked him if he was feeling all right, and Al just shrugged and mumbled an unconvincing "Fine." His customary charm and cheer had been all but extinguished. Dylan asked Kate if she knew what was bothering Al, whether the pain was beginning to get worse or what, but she didn't know any more about it than Dylan did. She'd asked, too, but Al didn't want to talk about it, and that was that. It gave Dylan another reason to go up to Meralta just to get away from the gloom.

But it also made him worry. Al had never hidden things from them before. Even when the doctors had delivered their crushing news, Al had kept up his spirits. It just wasn't like him to get depressed. But Dylan had to admit he was certainly entitled to.

The next week, Dylan sensed a new tension in the air, some sort of veiled argument going on between his parents. He could see it in the way they looked at each other, in the way they would slam doors and move objects a bit more roughly than usual. Something was smoldering under the surface, but when Dylan would ask them what was wrong, they would exchange glances waiting for each other to give the secret away. "Nothing," they would finally tell him. "Nothing."

"Come on. What are you hiding from me?" Dylan would demand.

Glaring at each other, Al and Kate would change the subject. "How's the film coming along?" Al would inquire. And Dylan would shake his head and mutter an answer, all the while wondering what in hell was going on.

"Let's take a walk," Al suggested one afternoon when Dylan got home from school.

"Sure," Dylan said gladly. Al's wanting to go out had to be a good sign. He hadn't been going out much at all lately. Now he looked more alive than he had in days. But on the other hand, when Al proposed a walk, it usually meant he had something serious on his mind, and that made Dylan slightly apprehensive.

"Going for a walk" always meant going for a ride first. There was really nowhere to walk in the neighborhood. They got into the Blazer, and Dylan drove toward the beach. As they rode in silence, Al suddenly looked worried, agitated, weary again. Whatever it is, Dylan thought, maybe getting it out in the open will do him some good.

They had the beach to themselves. It was usually empty that time of year, too cold to swim or sunbathe and not as good for surf fishing as the next cove up. They got out of the truck and walked toward the shore. Suddenly Al stopped short. "Listen, I think I'd better say what I have to right now instead of stalling," he began. Dylan sensed this was going to be difficult.

"You know I'm dying," Al said flatly over the rumble of the waves. "I've tried not to kid you about it. I think it's better to let you know what's going on rather than hide things from you. Always have. You know that."

Dylan wanted to say something, but he could feel the pressure building in his eyes and throat, and he knew whatever he said would come out squeaky and choked and strange. What he wanted to say was that his father's honesty was one of the things he loved him for, but he didn't say that or anything else. He just nodded and looked down at the sand.

"I've had a lot of time to think lately," Al said. "And read. As you've noticed. Anyway, what it all comes down to is that I'd rather go out a human being instead of waiting around until I'm a suffering vegetable making everybody else miserable."

Dylan looked up. Al stared him straight in the eye. "Right," he said. "I'm talking about killing myself."

Difficult? This was going to be impossible. Dylan felt as though he'd been punched in the head. Stunned, he stared back at the sand, as though it might have words scratched in it, the words he couldn't begin to find inside his brain.

"I'm not saying today or tomorrow or the day after," Al went on. "But I am saying soon. I'd like to work up a plan, put everything in order, help you and your mom get ready to live without me, share some good times together. Then I'd like to find some quick and painless way to die, without hanging on and becoming a goddamned nuisance."

Dylan had trouble breathing. As the idea of his father's killing himself began to sink in, it somehow suffocated him, made him feel as though he were drowning. "Have you told Mom?" he gasped.

Al nodded and looked away.

"What does she think?"

"She's against it." Al pushed some sand around with the side of his shoe. "We've had arguments about it. Big ones. Fights. You noticed." He looked up. "What do you think?"

"I'm against it, too," Dylan said so forcefully he surprised himself.

Al kicked a beer can out of the way. "This doesn't seem to be a popular idea."

Dylan felt his anger rising. "You can't just kill yourself," he insisted. "You can't."

"Of course I can," Al snapped. "Easiest thing in the world. What you mean is I shouldn't."

"Okay. You shouldn't."

"Why not? Why shouldn't I?"

Dylan knew Al would get around to that question. "Because it's not right," he replied, realizing it wasn't anywhere near enough of an answer. "There are other people depending on you."

"You and your mom?"

"Right."

"You can't depend on me much longer, Dyl. At some point I'm not going to be around no matter whether I kill myself or the cancer does. Wouldn't it be better if you knew exactly when I'd be gone, rather than have it drag on and on?"

"No," Dylan said firmly.

"I'm trying to be open, honest, about this. Would you rather I killed myself without warning you?"

"I would rather you quit talking about killing yourself. What if they suddenly found a cure for what you've got? If you kill yourself, you take that chance away."

"With this kind of cancer, that chance is about as close to zero as anything gets. I'm not even sure I'd want to be cured once this thing starts eating away at me. Oh, hell, yes, I probably would. I guess I just don't believe all those films where the cavalry comes rushing in at the last instant."

"Come on," Dylan said. "You've *been* that cavalry. How do you think all those people felt just before you rushed in and took them out of all those burning buildings?"

A wisp of a smile crossed Al's face. "You should've been on the debating team."

"Anyway, isn't suicide illegal?"

"Oh, yeah," Al said thoughtfully. "But I don't happen to believe it's up to the state to make that decision for you. It's your own life. If you want to kill yourself slowly by drinking or smoking, there's no law against that." He looked out toward the water. "I don't know, maybe there should be. I just want to go out with some dignity, among people I love, instead of writhing with pain and babbling like an idiot in some hospital or ambulance. Fair enough?"

"You talk as though it would be some sort of noble gesture to kill yourself," Dylan said bitterly. "An act of bravery."

"Hell, no! I don't think suicide's particularly noble. Or brave. Most people would probably say it's cowardly. But you know I've never given a damn for what people say. I just think this may be the right thing to do. Not for everybody—I'm not recommending it. But for me."

Dylan watched the waves roll in. They reminded him of a movie he'd seen where the hero committed suicide by walking straight out into the ocean until the sea swallowed him up. He could imagine his father doing something like that, something brave and grand, challenging the waves to take him under and be quick, damn it. But he could also imagine some of the emptiness he'd feel afterwards. It made him shudder.

Al's voice was choked, thick. "This is the toughest decision I've ever had to make."

Dylan smoothed a patch of sand with his foot to avoid meeting his father's eyes. "You don't have to make it."

"That's what makes it so tough."

"You don't have to give up. You could do what everybody else does. Fight back. Try to survive. Hope for a miracle."

"I'm not giving up. I'm trying the chemotherapy, and God knows that's not much fun. But sooner or later they're going to tell me it's not working, and I'm not going to kid myself. I've seen people roasted alive. I've seen people die of smoke inhalation. Not to mention all those old people I've known who live their deaths for years before they officially get around to dying. I've seen more death than most people. I know something about it."

He looked out at the horizon. "Look, the whole damned situation is so tricky. Most of philosophy is on the side of preserving human life at any cost. So is most of religion, sometimes with the added attraction of an afterlife. But you know I've never believed in religion, and personally I'm not at all sure people are best off hanging on and on. I'm beginning to think a lot of the philosophical arguments against suicide are just ways of rationalizing the philosophers' fear of death. And you know that's one fear I've never had."

Dylan fidgeted. "You can wait until things get worse, you know. You don't have to decide this now."

"Yeah, but I want to. What I really want to do is pick a good day to die and stick to it. I'd like to settle it before I get too damned miserable and weak to be able to do it. And I'd like to give you and Kate some time to recover. You're starting college in the fall, so I was thinking about late spring, after your graduation. You and your mom could begin to rearrange your lives before I go, and then you'd have the summer to get everything sorted out."

"God! You make it sound as though you were going on a business trip or something."

"Dylan, this is all new to me. It's not as though it's something I've had a lot of practice expressing. But I really think I'd enjoy the days I have left that much more if I knew when I was going to die."

"What if you change your mind?"

Al shrugged. "Then I change my mind. Anyhow, that won't happen. Not unless somebody gives me some awfully good argument."

Dylan tried desperately to think of one. "Look, say you pick a particular day to kill yourself, which is what you claim you want to do, right?"

Al nodded.

"Okay," Dylan went on, "but maybe you won't even live that long. The cancer could get worse. Or you could get run over by a car or something."

"Then I've done the best I could. Death wins. Death wins sooner or later anyway."

"Dad, please," Dylan begged, trying to hold back his tears. "Please don't do this."

Al lowered his voice. "I think I may have to."

They stood for what seemed like hours avoiding each other's glance. The waves came in and lapped at their shoes, and they drew back. "One more thing," Al said finally. "I haven't decided yet how I'm going to do this—or even *if* for sure—but I want you to know it won't have anything to do with fire. That's more or less my natural enemy, and it's a horrible way to die. I want to go out peacefully, or at least peacefully enough so that everybody else can rest easy. What I want to do is tell you how and when, maybe even have you there by my side. So if I get strong enough to go back on the job and then I die in a fire, believe me, it wasn't for lack of trying to stay alive."

"You still think you'll get back to the firehouse?"

"If I can get some of my strength back, damned right I will. It's what I do."

Dylan stared at Al. He was so damned brave. How could anyone live up to him? And now, how could anyone save him?

He put his hand on Dylan's shoulder. "Listen, until I get this all sorted out, this isn't something I want to get around. It's not an easy thing to understand . . ."

"That's for sure," Dylan interrupted.

". . . and I don't want to spend the rest of my days —'the rest of my days,' how dramatic—explaining myself to people. I'd like you not to talk about this with anybody except your mom and me."

Dylan nodded.

"I know it's hard to carry something like this around in your head without talking to anybody about it," Al went on, "but I have to ask you anyway. I didn't hide my cancer, and I'm not ashamed of it.

I'm not ashamed of this, either. If it's the right thing to do, it's the right thing to do. I just think it should be private. It's not something most people will understand. Okay?"

Dylan barely had the energy to nod. He felt his strength had ebbed away, drained out, deserted him. His muscles were limp. His eyes were overflowing.

Al gave him a sympathetic pat on the shoulder and started back toward the Blazer. Through his tears, Dylan looked down at the sand. The waves were coming in farther now, and with each new wash of water, his father's footprints were beginning to disappear.

Chapter Seven

DYLAN drove home utterly stupefied. In a way, he kept thinking, this was worse than if his father had already died. When somebody was dead—or dying—there wasn't much you could do but make the best of it.

But this! It was like the sickest joke of all time. How could you live with the knowledge your father was planning to kill himself and not do something to stop him? Yet what could you do, really? Beg? Plead? Watch him every minute, every second?

The road was the last thing on Dylan's mind. Twice he had to veer off at the last instant, slamming on the brakes, when his thoughts brought him split seconds away from accidents. Al didn't say anything either time. He just gave Dylan a glance of mild disappointment, as if to say he understood why Dylan was upset but it would be nice if he would keep his mind on his driving.

But Al couldn't understand, not totally, Dylan kept thinking. He couldn't understand, or he wouldn't do this. Pain or no pain, dignity or no dignity, how could anyone want to die—to leave friends, family—a moment earlier than he absolutely had to?

When they got home Al disappeared into the bedroom to rest before dinner. Dylan went into the kitchen. His mother was bending over the sink, washing lettuce for salad. Usually she tore greens gently into bite-sized pieces, but now she was ripping them angrily, abruptly, into big hunks.

"He told me," Dylan said.

63

"I know," Kate replied, concentrating on the lettuce to avoid looking at him.

"How do you feel about it?"

"How do you think I feel about it?"

"The way I do, probably."

"And how's that?"

Dylan searched for the right expression. "Helpless."

Kate turned toward him. "Good word choice," she said bitterly. "I'd give you an A."

"You think there's any way we can stop him?"

Kate shook her head. "Has anybody ever been able to stop him once he gets an idea in his head? The only person who'll be able to make him change his mind is Al Donaldson."

"We could argue with him. Make him try to see he's wrong."

Kate exhaled wearily. "Dylan, I've *been* arguing with him. I've been *fighting* him. I'm worn out."

"Maybe I should try."

"Sure. You could nag him. We both could. It might work. But do you want him to spend the last days of his life being nagged?"

Dylan shrugged. "We could try it for a little while. Maybe he'd come around."

"Maybe." Kate dried her hands on a dish towel. "But do we really know he's wrong? Obviously this is wrong as far as we're concerned, but maybe for him it's not. He knows how he feels. He knows things we don't."

"What are we going to do, then?" Dylan demanded. "Just sit around while he sets up a plan to kill himself and let him go through with it and then live happily ever after? We should at least try *something*."

His mother slouched against the refrigerator, her energy entirely drained. "I know, Dylan. I know how you feel. But I don't know what the right thing is. How many times does anybody ever have to deal with something like this? We don't teach it in the public schools, I know that."

"That's for sure."

"He realizes what an incredible burden he's laying on us. He's asking us to help him kill himself. And I don't want to. He's brave enough for it, but I'm not. I told him yesterday, if he's going to do it, he should leave us out of it. But now the more I think about it, the more I think if he really is going to kill himself, maybe I *would* like to know about it."

They stared at each other without saying anything. "What about getting him to see a psychiatrist or a psychologist or somebody? It seems to be helping that kid in my class who tried to kill himself."

Kate sighed. "Dylan, give me *some* credit. I've suggested that a dozen times. And Al did talk to a counselor at the hospital when he was so depressed. But he doesn't look at this idea—this plan of his—as something he wants to change. He says it's just an improvement on what's going to happen anyway." She shook her head. "Maybe the best thing to do is just let it ride. Wait and see what happens. You know Al. If we keep bringing it up, arguing with him, he's liable to fight back, push harder for what he wants just to prove he's right. He hasn't made the final decision yet. Maybe we should just let it go for now."

"Except if we do, he may think we approve of the idea."

"Oh, he knows how we feel, all right. He won't kid himself about that."

Dylan shrugged. "I still wish there were some way . . ."

"If you think of one, for godsake let me know. In the meantime, all I'm trying to do is put this whole mess out of my head. How about drying that lettuce for me?" She left the room.

So much for the discussion about Al. Dylan dumped the lettuce into the salad spinner and yanked angrily on the cord, so hard he was afraid it might break. He hoped Kate was right: sooner or later his father had to realize this suicide plan of his was absolutely crazy.

And what made it all crazier as far as Dylan was concerned was that he had to go on living, go through the motions of daily life, as if nothing had changed. At least with his closest friends, and especially with Barbra, he'd been able to count on a little sympathy when he brought up the subject of his dying father. Of course, the rest of the world didn't give a damn. You couldn't tell your physics teacher you were having trouble concentrating because you were thinking about how weak your father looked that morning, and you couldn't use your father's condition as an excuse for not knowing your lines in media class.

But this suicide business made things ten times worse. Dylan kept wondering if he'd return home someday to find his father had killed himself. That wasn't the way the plan was supposed to work, but it worried and frightened him all the same. And not being able to talk about it tore him up inside. He wanted to tell Barbra about it, but telling her would've betrayed Al's trust, and who knew?—Al might well change his mind. But *not* telling her made him feel he was keeping secrets and betraying *her*. The only thing he could do was try to forget all about it, live day by day, put the whole thing out of his mind. Which was impossible. When Al went out on an errand, Dylan would wonder if he'd ever come back. When they played chess, Dylan would wonder if this game would be the very last one ever.

And Kate kept nagging him. She wanted him to give up gliding for a while. The way she saw it, he was downright irresponsible to even think about jumping off cliffs when his father was in such a lousy state. It got to the point where Dylan almost felt guilty about flying, but he did it anyway. He had to— not only for himself, but for the film.

That Sunday he was supposed to try some practice runs for the cameras, and he invited Barbra to come along and watch. Since he had to drive all the way to Meralta to get her, he was up even earlier than usual, before the sun had made the slightest impact on the darkness. He and Barbra joked about how romantic it was. Even the McDonald's they stopped at had a certain charm at that hour of the morning. They watched dawn break as they wolfed down their Egg McMuffins.

When they got to the ledge, the inseparable Sean and Yolanda were already arguing about where to set up the video equipment. Short, stocky Sean insisted the camera was too close to the edge, but tall, fearless Yolanda, formidable in her jump suit, flatly overruled him. Meanwhile, Jay, man of few words, made goofy faces to let Dylan know he thought Barbra wasn't bad-looking at all. "You're damn near the only thing he talks about anymore," Jay informed her.

"All good stuff, I hope," she said a little awkwardly.

Jay tipped his hat and made a low bow. "Definitely."

Sean came over to join them. "You should find a boyfriend who's not into doing strange things at ridiculous hours of the morning," he told Barbra with a yawn.

"Ridiculous?" Yolanda hollered from the edge. "Six A.M. is ridiculous?"

"Even the birds aren't up yet," Sean shouted back.

"Yeah, but the light's fantastic," Yolanda proclaimed. "Look at that sky! Besides, you're just the writer. You don't have to be here."

"Ha!" Sean replied. "You held a gun to my head!"

Dylan and Barbra exchanged scowls. It wasn't really anybody's fault that they didn't find Sean's joke funny.

"Well, she did," Sean went on lamely. "A shotgun mike, anyway."

Dylan changed the subject. "Who's going down in the Blazer, and who's staying up here?"

"We'll stay," Sean said. "We're all set up, at least until our great director knocks the camera off the cliff. I can hardly move this time of morning, anyway."

"Looks like I take the truck, then," Jay said. "Barb?"

"I'll stay up here," she said, putting her camera to her eye. "I want to shoot from down there later, though."

"Hell!" Jay said. "Looks like I'm one lonely errand boy." He got into the truck.

"Don't forget to put up the streamers," Dylan reminded him.

"Forget? Hell, Dylan, sometimes you really make me feel brilliant, you know?" Jay grunted, and drove away.

As Dylan set up the glider, Barbra took pictures and asked questions. Dylan usually enjoyed teaching her things she didn't know, but today he found it a little distracting. Normally he would put every bit of his concentration into connecting the wires and tightening the turnbuckles and fastening the pins. Now, part of his mind was diverted to explaining things to Barbra. And another part kept drifting uncontrollably to morbid thoughts about his father. Don't let it get you, he told himself. Concentrate. Concentrate.

"It's beautiful," Barbra said, snapping a picture as he tightened the last cable. "So fragile. Hard to believe it'll actually hold you up."

Dylan grinned. "Wait and see."

He avoided talking while he made the final inspection. Everything checked out. Barbra reloaded her camera and joined Sean and Yolanda at the edge of the cliff.

"Make it good, champ!" Yolanda shouted. "We're rolling!"

Dylan nodded sharply. He blew Barbra a kiss the way he imagined Lindbergh might have done it. Then he nosed the wing into the wind and made his run and leap.

It was as magical as ever. The sail filled, and Dylan floated through the air. He kept his descent slow, hoping to find a thermal and make a partial turn so he could gain altitude, give his friends on the ledge a better angle, maybe even wave to them. But what looked at first like a thermal was only some turbulence he had to fight off for a couple of seconds. Gil had warned him about those—"fakoes," he called them.

Dylan made a forty-five degree turn, but with the sail above him there was no way he could catch sight of Barbra and the others, and with the turbulence, he didn't want to risk turning farther and having to fight the wind to get back on course. He veered into the wind and caught a little roller coaster bump from another patch of turbulence. Then he watched the streamers and prepared for his landing.

He touched down a few yards from the Blazer. Another fine flight, except for those little whorls of air, except that he'd been hoping for those thermals and some extra height and time aloft. Not perfect, but not bad. Seven on a scale of ten.

"This is almost getting to be boring," Jay told him as they loaded the glider into the truck.

Dylan shrugged. "Not for me."

When they got back to the cliff, Barbra looked ecstatic. "It was wonderful," she told Dylan, squeezing his hands. "I've never seen this except on television. You look so free out there."

"You should try it."

"I'm almost tempted. It looks glorious. I want to see it from below this time."

"Us, too," Yolanda agreed, lugging the camera and recorder toward the truck. "This time I want suspense, trouble, danger in the air. Action, for godsake."

"Lay off," Dylan said irritably. "If that's what you're looking for, hire a professional stuntman."

"She doesn't mean get yourself killed, Dylan," Sean put in. "Yolanda's just trying to make the most visual movie she can."

"Why doesn't she just go out and shoot accidents on the freeway?" Jay inquired.

"That's an idea. Maybe I can work it into the script," Sean answered sarcastically as he put the Blazer into gear and drove off.

"Looks like I'll be alone again," Jay said, yawning. "Wouldn't mind being alone with that Barbra of yours, I'll tell you. Not half bad, and rich besides."

"Hey, enough of that 'rich' business," Dylan said, continuing his inspection.

"Never hurts to have money," Jay said. "Comes in handy now and then." He leaned against the station wagon and tried to grab a quick nap.

A few minutes later, Dylan was ready with the glider. "See if they're down there," he asked.

Jay shuffled over to the edge, looked down, and gave the high sign. Dylan nosed the glider into the wind, ran, and jumped.

Again the split second of fear ran through him, and again the sail buoyed him up. He aimed for some dust motes that seemed to be rising. His guess was right: a thermal, a draft of warm air that carried him gently upward.

He rode the thermal until the sail rose above the level of the ledge. This was where you had to watch yourself; the winds could be exceptionally tricky. Surprised to see Dylan up so high, Jay began yelling and waving his hat like a little kid. Dylan waited to wave back until he was safely out of the thermal and descending smoothly again.

He was wondering what he could do to give the groundlings a special thrill when he hit another one of those fakoes. Nothing special; he just rode it out and continued his lazy descent. He decided to try a couple of ninety-degree turns for practice and show.

The first two felt fine, a quick sharp left and an easy flowing right that worked the way they were supposed to. He headed left again, but as he moved across the control bar, he ran into more of that turbulence. With his weight far to the side of the glider, the sail began to tilt over, and he had to fight his way along the control bar to get it back into line.

At the other end of the bar he realized he'd overcompensated. The glider was facing the wrong way; he'd have to correct his heading at least ninety degrees to reach the clearing. But as he shifted his weight back along the bar, he saw that he was dropping fast. Not dangerously fast, just annoyingly fast. Too fast. He'd misjudged his altitude. There was no way he could make the clearing now.

All he could do was pick the best alternative. One patch of scrub seemed lower than the rest, and Dylan headed for it. He tried to slow his descent as much as possible, hoping that the gentlest of landings would do no damage to the glider—or its pilot.

He outfinessed himself. In cutting his speed, he undershot the low brush by about ten yards. He came down in scraggly foliage a couple of feet high, managed to plant his feet on solid ground instead of brush, and then watched helplessly as the sail came down behind him in the scrub and made a sickening ripping sound.

"No! No! Don't get up!" he heard Yolanda yell. "Stay down! We can use this footage!"

The hell with that, Dylan thought. He unfastened his harness, stood up, and tried to rock the sail out of the brush as gently as he knew how.

"No, don't!" Yolanda yelled, and then he heard Barbra shout, "Dylan, are you okay?"

71

"Yeah," he said disgustedly, without even turning around. Some way to impress your girlfriend, he thought, reddening with anger and embarrassment.

"You shouldn't've gotten up," Yolanda said, moving in for a close-up of the torn sail. "I might've been able to use that scene."

"So damned sorry," Dylan snapped.

"You okay?" Barbra asked with an exceptionally anxious look on her face.

"Yeah," Dylan said sheepishly. "Yeah. No big deal. I think the sail ripped, is all."

"Well, it can't be a virgin all its life," Sean said, trying to inject some humor.

"What happened?" Barbra asked.

"Misread the wind. Also my altitude," Dylan muttered, looking at the sail. "Damn. This thing is *really* torn."

"What do you do about that?" Barbra wondered.

"I sure don't fly it," Dylan said. "Usually they can make a patch."

"How long'll that take?" Yolanda asked. "We were supposed to shoot this for real next week."

Dylan shrugged.

"So that's it for today, right?" Sean said.

"I'd say so, yeah," Dylan replied.

Sean slapped him on the back. "Listen, don't take it so hard. No big problem. I'll go move the truck up here so you won't have to carry the thing so far."

"Good idea," Dylan said. Sean and Yolanda tramped off through the brush toward the Blazer.

Barbra took a deep breath. "I guess it's not as easy as it looks."

Dylan shook his head. "Nothing ever is," he said ruefully. At which the serious-eyed Barbra screwed up her face, stuck out her tongue, and blasted forth a Bronx cheer that sounded like the world's wettest fart.

Dylan laughed in spite of himself. It was impossible to stay gloomy with Barbra's radiant smile right there in front of him demonstrating that things weren't so bad. "You win," he said, putting his arm around her shoulders. "Can't even have a little self-pity around here."

Chapter Eight

"**H**OW long will it take to fix?" Dylan asked the repairman.

"The sail, figure about a week. The bent strut, longer. Depends how soon we can get the part. You have to take it easy with these things. They're not meant for crash landings."

You're telling me, Dylan thought. The repairs were going to take a good hunk of his savings. And the incident hadn't exactly improved his "Mr. Careful" reputation at home. When she heard the news, his mother got totally exasperated even though Dylan pointed out that her wish had come true: he wouldn't be flying for a while. Al just said something like "Accidents will happen," but he did add that he hoped Dylan wasn't trying to show off or anything. Dylan blushed a little when he answered of course not.

The repair shop was halfway to L.A., so it was almost dinnertime when Dylan pulled the Blazer into his driveway. A newish Toyota Celica was parked there; he wondered whose it could be. Then he heard the sound of jazz, a clarinet and a sax, emerging from the house, and he figured he could make a pretty good guess.

Dylan tracked the sweet, sad music to the den. Barbra and his father were trading solos. She grinned at Dylan as Al fluffed a couple of notes, and Al shrugged in time with the music as if to ask what anybody could expect from someone so wildly out of practice. He ended the piece with an intricate little flourish, and Dylan applauded. Barbra and Al shared the same smug, proud look.

"Thank you, thank you," Al said, bowing grandly.

"Donations are always appreciated," Barbra added.

"How'd you get down here?" Dylan asked.

"Surprise! I passed my driver's test at lunchtime!"

"Congratulations."

"So naturally I rushed right over. I forgot you'd be taking care of your crippled wing."

"But Coleman Hawkins Junior here just happened to bring her saxophone along. Somehow she lured my clarinet out of retirement," Al said. "You have to admit, I'm not bad."

"You never were," Dylan said. "Why'd you ever give it up?"

"I don't know. It just sort of happened. Most of the guys in that band I used to fool around with moved away."

"What we need now is a drummer, a bassist, and a piano player," Barbra said. "Know anybody?"

Dylan shook his head. "Sorry."

"There are a couple of new guys down at the firehouse," Al said. "I think one of them plays drums with a rock band."

Barbra squinched up her face in disapproval.

"You never know," Al said. "Some of these rock guys are pretty damned good musicians."

"Mostly they're pretty damned loud musicians," Barbra replied.

"Well, I'll check around," Al said. "Meanwhile, if you want to borrow any of those records, feel free. Now I'll leave you two in peace." He turned to Dylan. "Oh, by the way, Barbra's staying for dinner."

"Great," Dylan said a little uneasily as his father walked upstairs. He was glad to see Al in high spirits for a change, but he wished he'd been the one to invite Barbra to stay. In fact, he wished he'd been the one playing music with her. There was something wonderful about two people in sync like that, something almost sexy, that made him a little jealous.

76

"See, you do have a thing going," he half teased.

"Oh, come on," she said, shaking spit from the sax.

"You have to," he insisted. "Nobody—but nobody —has ever been allowed to borrow those records of his. It's absolutely unheard of. If you ask why, he'll give you his standard speech about how somebody once dropped a lampshade on one of his out-of-print Sidney Bechets."

"Well, I'll keep the records a long way from any lampshades."

Dylan was about to tell her to be sure to keep her stylus clean, something else his father was fanatic about, but the idea suddenly crept into his head that maybe Al was only letting her borrow the records because he didn't really care what happened to them— after all, he wasn't going to be around much longer himself. Dylan changed the subject. "Is that your car out there?"

"My father's. He's got a company car, so he's letting me use this one."

"Nice. So it's as good as yours."

"Yeah, more or less."

"You like driving it?"

"It's funny, I really thought I'd hate it. I mean, I didn't even like riding in cabs back home. You just missed being in an accident every time you came to an intersection. But out here, I don't know, there's something about it . . ."

"What?"

"Freedom, I guess. Like your glider. You just get into your chariot and point it in the right direction, and there you are. You can go anywhere without having to stand around and wait on streetcorners, and you get your own choice of music. If it weren't for all the nutty drivers on the road, it'd be wonderful."

"See? You're turning into a regular Californian," Dylan said.

"Yeah, it's terrible. All I kept thinking about on

77

the way down here was taping some jazz cassettes for the player. My dad's cassettes are all classical, which is okay, but, you know, may as well go first class."

"Tape yourself. Then you can listen to your own music while you drive."

"I'd never have the guts for that," Barbra said, scowling. "What's the word on the glider?"

"Don't ask."

"Bad, huh?"

Dylan nodded.

"Maybe you should trade it in for some drums, take some lessons, and join our little combo."

"I wouldn't have the guts for *that*. Besides, with my luck, I'd probably poke a hole in them with the drumsticks."

"Oh, come on. Cheer up," she said, touching his face and then wandering over to his father's trophy case. Dylan watched as she stood there and gawked. "Unbelievable," she muttered, moving along the shelves and leaning forward to read some of the inscriptions. "I knew your dad was a fireman, but somehow I never dreamed of anything like this."

"It's not that he's vain about them or anything," Dylan told her.

"Yeah, I know. I started looking at them when we first came down here, and he kind of pushed me away."

"The display was my mom's idea, years ago. It's more or less a running gag in the family that if she'd known Dad would turn into such a great fireman, she never would've started this."

"You should be proud. It's the first time I've ever seen trophies that actually *mean* something. You know, people put up their awards for winning tennis matches or golf tournaments, or, I don't know, selling fifty million dollars worth of insurance or something. Every one of these is for helping people."

She was eyeing the trophies with such admiration and fondness Dylan couldn't help but feel proud, but he also felt that twinge of jealousy again, as if he wished she were admiring *his* trophies. But if he'd had any, which he didn't, they'd be for surfing or gliding or acting or some dumb thing—not even up there in the fifty-million-dollars-worth-of-insurance class.

"Unbelievable!" Barbra exclaimed. "He ran into a burning building and risked his life to save two old people and a baby in a crib? How many people ever do anything like that?"

A shiver ran down Dylan's spine. He wished she'd stop. It was too painful. Yes, his father had saved plenty of lives, but now, when it really counted, who could save *him?*

"Aren't you proud of him?" she asked.

"Of course I'm proud of him."

"You have a funny way of showing it."

"Barbra, look: there aren't going to *be* any more trophies, unless they give him one for his whole career."

The sudden wetness in her eyes showed that she understood. She went over to the record shelves and sat down on the floor. Crossing her legs, she tilted her head to one side so she could read the jacket edges. It wasn't nearly as big a collection as the one Dylan had seen on her wall, but from the look on her face, most of the records were new to her. "Put this one on," she said, handing Dylan a beat-up old Louis Armstrong album. "God, Al's got some great stuff here. A *lot* of these are out of print."

"They're in good shape, too," Dylan said, carefully sliding the disc from its inner sleeve and putting it on the turntable. "He's a nut about cleaning them, keeping your fingerprints off them, using this static gun to keep them from getting dusty. The day he finally let me play his records himself, I think he was

79

more worried than the day I started driving. You want to sit on the couch or the floor?"

"I'm sort of in a floor mood."

"We've got some cushions. I'll get 'em out." He flipped a lever to start the turntable, and while he was dragging two big beanbags out of the closet, the brassy tones of Armstrong's cornet sliced through the air.

They lay back on the cushions. Dylan had heard the music before, remembered it vaguely, but he had never really paid it much attention. "Listen to that," Barbra said softly, leaning forward as if it would help her hear better. Dylan listened, but the music was too raw for his mood. The powerful cornet seemed almost to reach out and punch him in the ears. And the record sounded kind of scratchy and fuzzy, which didn't help. It wasn't that Dylan disliked it; it was just that he didn't want to hear that particular kind of thing just then. Armstrong was aggressive, defiant, soaring; Dylan wanted peace, tranquility, romance.

But Barbra's face was so full of excitement, it said "Great, huh?" without uttering a word. Dylan smiled and nodded half-heartedly. He knew she could tell his soul wasn't really into it.

"Incredible," Barbra murmured, and Dylan nodded agreement. He was concentrating not on the music but on her hair, on the way one strand coiled around the back of her ear like some amorous snake about to whisper something only she was meant to hear. He watched the way her nostrils flared ever so slightly as she breathed, the way the skin at the corner of her eye crinkled into little radiating lines as she smiled, the way the pupils of her eyes magically danced without actually moving. She stared back with a scolding look, as if to tell him to concentrate on the music and not on her, but her presence overwhelmed him. He leaned forward and kissed her on the mouth.

Barbra gently pushed him away, with a look that seemed to say "not now," that she was concentrating on Satchmo and didn't want to be disturbed. Dylan moved away, a little embarrassed. He just couldn't get into the music, and his thoughts wandered all over the map—to his crippled glider, to Barbra's gleaming eyes, to his father's happy look just now, something very rare with him these days. When the number finished, Barbra gave him a kiss—a very motherly one, he thought, but he'd take it—and told him there was a time for everything. Then the next cut began, and she moved away, leaning forward and losing herself in the music once more.

Dinner was what Barbra later called a "California-style meal": avocado salad and a quiche Al had made, along with a dessert of leftover carrot cake. Dylan was glad to see how quickly his mother took to Barbra, especially once they began discussing the differences between schools in New York and California. Barbra thought there was more academic competition in New York, but she admitted it might have been because she'd gone to an expensive private school. Everybody in New York seemed to agree that most of the public schools were the pits—something Kate found hopelessly sad even though Barbra said it was just a fact of life.

And Dylan couldn't help but notice the way Barbra hit it off again with Al. They began with typical small talk about kinds of jazz they liked, and soon Barbra started drawing other things out of him, personal things like when and how he'd learned to play, and what had gotten him interested in jazz in the first place—things Dylan himself had either never found out or had long since forgotten.

Over coffee, Barbra asked Al how he'd become a fireman. "That's what everybody would like to know," Al said with his customary smile, launching into his standard explanation about his days as a philosophy student and the small demand for philosophers. Having heard this many, many times before, Dylan simply watched Barbra's reaction. If he didn't know better he would've almost thought she had a crush on Al. And Al's illness, his weakness, seemed to have disappeared for the moment. Dylan's useless jealousy flared up again.

Afterward, Barbra and Dylan decided to go down to the cove. Barbra said she was too nervous to drive in front of Dylan yet, especially at night, so he took the wheel of the Celica.

"Terrific car," he told her, pushing it into a curve.

"Me, I wouldn't know. Picking out stuff like this is a personal specialty of my father's. God knows where he learned it. Oh, I almost forgot." She twisted around and took a flat package from the backseat.

"What's that?"

"Eyes on the road. You'll find out soon enough."

"Surprise, huh?"

Barbra flashed a mysterious smile. "You'll see once we get there." Dylan stomped so hard on the accelerator that Barbra had to ask him to slow down.

The beach was deserted. The night was clear and dark. When Dylan parked, Barbra handed him the package. He could barely see it. "Where's the inside light switch?" he asked, searching the dashboard.

Barbra laughed. "I have no idea. That's one thing you don't need to know on the driver's test."

"Well, you can always do it this way." He opened the door a crack. The ignition reminder buzzed, and he took the key out to silence it.

Barbra watched expectantly as he unwrapped the package and slid out what was inside. It was a real surprise, all right: a big black-and-white photo of Dylan soaring through the air beneath the giant wing of the glider. It sent a shimmer of joy up his spine. "It's gorgeous."

"I was going to get a frame, but I didn't have time. I mounted it, though."

"It's incredible. Makes me look like I know what I'm doing. How'd you get the sky so dark?"

"Professional secret."

Dylan kept staring at it and shaking his head. Barbra was beaming, too, delighted at his delight. He leaned over and gave her a deep kiss, and this time she didn't push him away.

He pulled the door shut. The light went out. She was right. There was a time for everything.

Chapter Nine

TO JUDGE by his spirits, Al had the cancer all but licked. He was going back to the firehouse now, mornings only, just for paperwork, but it was almost like the old days. He'd bring home stories about the old man who had somehow managed to run eighteen electrical appliances from one socket without even paying for the power or the woman who had taught her cat how to turn on the oven while she was at work, and the old glow would be in his eyes as he described them. His afternoon naps were getting shorter. He was practicing his clarinet for the first time in ages. He was reading books that didn't happen to deal with death. And though he was losing hair and weight from his chemotherapy and his cancer, he had stopped complaining about his aches and pains. If he was still contemplating suicide, he was doing a hell of a good job of keeping it to himself.

Dylan was thankful for it. Being able to get his mind off his father's problems, even for a little while, was a relief. He had enough problems of his own to take care of, especially with Yolanda, who was giving him a crash course in just how hard filmmaking could be. The lanky perfectionist thought absolutely nothing of demanding "take" after "take" of a shot she wanted. It wasn't so terrible the first six or seven times, but it got to be pretty tiresome by the twentieth or thirtieth. Between each repetition, there was usually a long, boring wait for a change in the light or for somebody's makeup to be freshened up, or for some adjustment to the camera. Dylan's patience began to wear thin. He wondered if he was really cut out to be an actor after all.

The toughest time was the morning they filmed the opening sequence. It was a simple shot, Yolanda kept telling everybody. Dylan would start as a speck way out on the water and then surf straight into camera. An easy one, she kept saying. Nothing to it.

That was just to keep the cast—in this case, Dylan—and crew from getting worried. The shot was about as easy as putting a surfboard through the eye of a needle. Not only did Dylan have to hold a line straight toward the camera all the way from God knew where, but he also had to maintain what Sean's screenplay called "a grim, fixed expression," which was not the easiest thing to do while you were concentrating on your surfing. Also he and the cameraman had to turn away from each other at the *very* last second to avoid a collision that would send a few thousand bucks worth of equipment into the water. So no matter what Yolanda said, it was anything but simple.

And just to make things interesting, the water on the day of the shoot was as cold as a gym teacher's heart, with decent waves coming along maybe once every ten minutes. Dylan had to go out in his specially painted wetsuit, wait patiently while his fingers and toes turned blue, then catch a wave and ride it perfectly with that "grim, fixed expression"— which had literally frozen on his face. They started at seven A.M., but by ten Yolanda still hadn't made a single shot that worked, and then she began to get dissatisfied with the light and finally called it a day. Dylan couldn't stop shivering for an hour.

After dinner that evening, Al announced it was time for a little family talk, and Dylan's shivers came back again. Al's tone was downright cheerful, but there was something in it that made Dylan absolutely certain something terrible was about to be sprung on him.

They moved to the living room. Dylan and Kate sat on the couch. "Well, I've decided," Al declared, settling into his recliner.

Dylan and Kate glanced at each other with the resigned certainty that they knew what Al was talking about. "June thirtieth," he announced.

"For what?" Kate demanded, challenging him to come out and say what she and Dylan already were sure of.

"To end my life," Al said simply.

Kate scowled. "*That* again," she muttered, as if it were some persistent insect that kept coming back to sting her.

"It'll give you both plenty of time to make plans," Al pointed out with a calmness that Dylan envied and hated. "You'll be able to get things straightened out before the school year begins again. Besides, if the doctors are right, I'll still be in halfway decent shape by then."

"Why don't you make it the Fourth of July?" Kate said sarcastically. "We'll shoot off firecrackers."

Al stayed cool. "The thirtieth of June seems reasonable enough. It's a Saturday."

"Dad, you can't do this," Dylan blurted out, feeling foolish the instant the words crossed his lips.

"I've been trying the idea out for more than a week now," Al explained in that patient way. of his. "I picked the day last weekend, and I've been living with it ever since." He paused reflectively. "It feels good. It's as though I know I have control over my life again."

"But that's just an illusion," Kate said.

Al shrugged. "It's a damned good one. Even when the pains rip through me now, I don't get depressed. I hope somebody noticed, I've been a hell of a lot easier to live with lately. And it's been a hell of a lot easier living with myself."

"Why do you have to make this decision now?"

Kate demanded. "If you have to pick a time to die, can't you at least wait until your pain gets worse?"

"No. That's the whole point. I'm not picking a time to die. I'm deciding how long I have left to live. I'm going to do my damnedest to stick around until June thirtieth. If I make the decision on the basis of how I'm feeling, who knows? I might want to die even sooner. Spare myself some agony."

"Not you," Kate scoffed.

"Look, I know how brave you think I am, and I'm proud of it. But I've tried this idea on, and it seems to fit. If you've got any arguments I haven't heard, I'm willing to listen."

Dylan and Kate looked to each other for support, but neither knew what to say. Kate finally spoke in a somber, subdued tone. "Al, I still don't believe you can just take yourself away from us like this. Why can't you die naturally, the way everybody else does?"

"We've discussed this, Kate," Al said with some irritation. "I'm not everybody else. Besides, I won't be depriving you of much. A couple of months at most, and those couple of months I'd be mostly a feeble nuisance."

"I don't see how you can know that," Kate said.

"I don't see why you won't face up to it," Al replied.

There was a long silence. Dylan finally broke it. "Now that you've made up your mind, are you going to tell anyone else?"

"No," Al said firmly. "Maybe Dad and Mom later. I haven't decided that yet. Otherwise, no."

Dylan and Kate looked at each other in total frustration. "I guess I should tell you I'm just going to take a pretty stiff overdose of sleeping pills," Al added. "From what I've read, that seems to be the most painless way. You fall asleep, you die within half an hour or so, and supposedly you don't feel a thing."

Dylan flashed on his father taking pill after pill: toss and gulp, toss and gulp, toss and gulp. "Where's the dignity in that?" he demanded.

"Look, I didn't say my actual death would be pretty," Al replied. "Death usually isn't. What I'm talking about is what happens before I die. The way I live from now till then. You probably can't see this yet, but as the time gets closer, I think it'll be something we all can share."

"You mean we're supposed to *celebrate* your suicide?" Dylan asked in amazement.

Al smiled. "Yeah. Something like that."

"Well, I won't," Kate said, her voice breaking. "I won't."

Al flashed a big grin. "How about if we call it 'creative suicide'?"

"You know what I call it, Al? I call it horseshit!" She ran from the room, stormed up the stairs, and slammed a door.

Kate never acted like this. Dylan gave his father a frustrated look, then followed her upstairs. Standing outside the door to his mother's office, he could hear her crying. Wondering if he should intrude, he knocked gently. "It's me," he said softly.

With a catch in her voice, Kate told him to come in. She was dabbing at her teary eyes with a Kleenex. Dylan stuck his hands in his pockets and slumped against the wall. "I guess he didn't just forget all about it."

"No," Kate sobbed, shoving some school papers aside so she wouldn't drip on them.

"Creative suicide!" Dylan snorted. "It's so damned weird."

Kate nodded, dabbed. Dylan had never seen her look so forlorn, so helpless. "Maybe somebody else could get him to come to his senses," she said.

"We're not supposed to tell anybody else."

"I know. That's almost the worst part."

Dylan sighed. "Who knows? He's usually right about everything. Maybe he's right about this, too. Maybe we're just upset because he wants to do something we don't want him to. Something you're not supposed to."

"June thirtieth is so close," Kate mumbled.

"I know," Dylan said. "I know." He wished he had an answer, but he wasn't even sure he knew the question. He told his mother it would all work out, squeezed her hand, and left the room.

"Creative suicide," he muttered to himself as he lay back on his bed and stared at the ceiling. "Creative suicide." Well, if anybody could pull that off, Dylan thought through his tears, it would have to be Al Donaldson.

Chapter Ten

INCREDIBLY enough, Al *was* pulling it off. June thirtieth was getting closer and closer, the clock was running, time was ticking away, and yet Al was somehow orchestrating his life in a way that often made Dylan forget almost totally about his death. Yet death, and the suicide plan, were really an important part of it all, in ways Dylan sensed but didn't entirely understand.

It wasn't like one of those TV shows about a girl with leukemia who comes to realize the preciousness of life and spends her dying hours learning the names of flowers, or one of those movies about a football hero who gets struck down by multiple sclerosis and discovers the beauty in every mundane moment. Al didn't go around preaching any particular gospel of life. He just, well, *lived*. And despite his obviously increasing fatigue and pain, he acted, seemed—or else actually *was*—incredibly happy.

At one point his optimism became so intense that Dylan came right out and asked him what in hell he could possibly be so cheerful about. "What have I possibly got to worry about?" Al retorted. "Higher prices? Murderers on the loose? Nuclear warfare? Starving children? Ring-around-the-collar? In two months' time, none of it will have a damned thing to do with me." But Dylan knew that was only part of the story. Al had never been a worrier to begin with.

Kate had her own interpretation. To hear her tell it, in his stubbornness to prove himself right about his suicide plan, he had simply willed himself happy

—just as he intended to will himself dead. She claimed Al was "going around like a grinning idiot." But then Kate had been bitter ever since Al had set the date. She cast a pall over the dinner table with her sullen looks, she would make offhand remarks about how some people couldn't "just die away" from their problems, and when she and Al were doing something together like fixing dinner, she would stare daggers at him, as though she felt she could get him to reconsider his stand by acting even more mulish than he was. None of it worked. Al just continued on his merry way, refusing to let Kate get his spirits down, and trying his best, without much success, to get hers up again.

As for Dylan, he couldn't remember when his days had been so lively, so overwhelmingly full. It was as though time had been compressed somehow, collapsed into itself like a folding cup or a telescope so that it seemed twice as intense as usual. The moments Dylan anticipated—like a series of jazz concerts he and Barbra expected the world of—often turned out to be little more than holes in the fabric of time. But other things—spontaneous, unexpected things like an especially loving look from Barbra, or his day-long exhilaration at getting a scholarship to Stanford, or his nasty argument with Yolanda over why it actually had to be *his* hand stabbing the knife into the villain's throat in the film's exceptionally bloody and revolting special-effects close-ups—lingered in his brain for days.

His memory kept playing the damnedest tricks on him. Rooting around in his closet for his baseball glove, he'd run across the pint-sized bat Al had given him when he'd started Little League, and the recollections would flow down through his brain like hot fudge down a sundae. Or he'd catch some scent in the air, a fragrance he couldn't identify or place, and somehow it would trigger an intense reminiscence of the first time he and his parents had driven up to Yosemite. That sort of thing had happened before, of course, but now the memories were tempered by a dark tinge of sadness.

One study period at school he remembered one of his ninth-grade assignments. The topic was "If you learned you had only one month to live, what would you do?" The class brain had said he'd travel all over the world and see the relics of history's greatest civilizations. A girl who was big on pottery said she'd spend the month working on her most ambitious vase so she could leave something of herself behind for the ages. Good, sweet Julie wrote that she'd devote herself to trying to help other people ("And I know exactly how," Dylan remembered Jay snickering). And Jay, crazy Jay, said he'd tour the world in search of the perfect wave. He'd lifted the idea from a surfing movie he'd seen on TV. The teacher knew it and flunked him.

Dylan remembered how hard he'd racked his brain to come up with an answer to the question. He'd finally decided to be honest and write that he really didn't know what he'd do. Whatever he did, he wrote, it wouldn't make a whole lot of difference to him one way or the other, since he wouldn't be around to see how it came out. He thought he'd probably do pretty much what he normally did and take each day as it came, though (attempt at humor) he'd probably cut school a lot.

When his turn came to read his paper in class, he felt slightly embarrassed. After everybody else's noble statements, he knew he'd come off looking like a jerk. But he also felt his answer was a damn sight more honest than most of the others—after all, where was the "brain" going to get the money for all his traveling?

When he read his paper, there was absolutely no response from the class. They'd been treating death as either a great adventure or a big joke, and he was treating it matter-of-factly. The teacher gave him a low mark: the assignment wasn't really about death, she said, it was about living your life to the fullest.

Which seemed to be Al's attitude now. Certainly it was tough to stay gloomy for long with Al's enthusiasm around to infect you. Barbra certainly caught it. There was no longer any question that she and Dylan were in love, and they didn't make any effort to hide it. But there was also no question that she was crazy about his father. Now that she'd become a driver—almost a full-fledged Californian, as she boasted, and she'd quit smoking to help prove it—she had given up her volunteering at the hospital and was coming down to San Felipe almost every day after school to play sax alongside Al's clarinet. Dylan still felt that twinge of jealousy when he saw them in such harmony, almost reading each other's minds, but he also took pleasure in seeing the two people he loved most look so happy. There was only one thing that really bothered him.

"Are you going to tell her?" he asked his father one day as Barbra pulled out of the driveway.

"What are you? Mr. Gloom?" Al asked. "We just had a terrific session."

"Yeah. I heard. Are you going to tell her?"

Al shrugged.

"You want me to tell her?" Dylan asked.

Al shook his head. "No, it's up to me. I just never considered it."

"Maybe you ought to," Dylan said. "She thinks you're terrific. Imagine how she's going to feel on July first."

"She knows I've got terminal cancer."

"Yeah, and she knows terminal cases don't just end"—Dylan snapped his fingers—"like that. You ought to tell her."

"I want to keep this in the family. She's strong. She'll be able to handle it."

"She's like family. And she's had to handle this once already. Remember, her mother was stabbed to death?"

"Oh, yeah," Al said thoughtfully, his smile dimming a little. "Listen, I'll think about it. Incidentally, you've got one hell of a woman there." He clapped Dylan on the back and disappeared into the house. Well, Dylan thought, at least I tried.

As the school year hurtled toward graduation, that already-compressed time seemed to squeeze still tighter. There was the school picnic, where Dylan managed to drag Barbra aboard her first—and, she insisted afterward, last—roller coaster. There were the two proms, where first he, then she, as exotic specimens from those alien planets known as "rival schools," were pointedly snubbed as bunches of girls and guys gathered together to make snotty comments about them. The one thing there wasn't was hang gliding, because the strut part he needed was still out of stock at the factory. Considering Kate's mood, it was probably just as well.

But the high point of the year had to be the premiere of the media class senior film, *Revenge of the Surfer*, starring Dylan Donaldson as The Surfer. Omar Wo was the villain. Nobody really wanted the cliché of an oriental villain, but Omar had won the part in open tryouts and threatened to bitch to the school board about racial discrimination if they didn't let him do it. In a last-minute compromise, he agreed to play the role in a cowboy hat.

Omar was also the film's publicity director. He had plastered the school hallways with gory posters that made everybody want, as his able assistant Jay aptly put it, "either to see the film or to throw up." He had also planned a truly stupendous premiere for opening night. Somehow Omar had conned local businessmen into donating two huge spotlights, along with limousines, tuxes and gowns for the stars and the crew. The junior media class covered the event for the school radio and TV stations. Just like Hollywood, Omar kept saying, just like Hollywood.

Well, enough like Hollywood. Dylan had to make a grand entrance with his co-star Julie, who gave him a truly monumental kiss for the TV cameras and nearly fell out of her low-cut gown. As they walked down the aisle in the auditorium, she flashed her big bubbly smile at the audience. Then they went to sit down at the V.I.P. section near the front, where Barbra was waiting.

It was no contest, Dylan realized, wedging himself in between them. Julie kept thrusting her painted lips at him and asking stupid questions that she already knew the answers to. Barbra just sat there in calm anticipation, her amused smile making her unmadeup face glow from the inside. No contest.

Then the room went dark, the screen lit up, and The Surfer hurtled toward the audience with that grim, fixed expression. As he watched, Dylan maintained his own grim, fixed expression in exquisite agony at the thought of a few hundred friends, acquaintances, enemies, and people he didn't even know inwardly criticizing his performance up there on the screen. To his right, Julie kept leaning her breasts against his arm. To his left, Barbra kept squeezing his hand and sending out squeals of delight at the good parts.

When the gory stuff came on, Dylan felt uneasy. Yolanda had really, literally, poured on the blood. He hoped it wouldn't offend his father. After all, in the end it *hadn't* been his hand that had done the stabbing—though Yolanda had done a perfect job of making it look that way.

At the cast party afterward, everybody kept coming up and congratulating him. Even Kate forgot her gloom long enough to find a few kind words for his performance, and Al was so lavish with praise for everything from the acting to the costumes that he came close to overdoing it. People kept calling Dylan "star," asking him what it was like to do those love scenes with Julie (embarrassing, he wanted to admit, but he just shrugged), and telling him what a great future he had as an actor. The flattery made him feel uncomfortable—besides, if acting meant freezing in a wet suit and cracking up your glider, he'd find another profession pronto—but Barbra, beaming at his side, got him through the evening. Her natural radiance made him feel prouder than all the compliments put together, and in the end she valiantly rescued him from a barrage of cake throwing that broke out among members of the cast. *You're* the star, Dylan kept telling her as she picked the icing from his hair. A superstar, he decided, as they made love in the car afterward.

Then came graduation. Aside from the fact that he would be, at long last, leaving Mission Margarita High once and for all, it was nothing special to Dylan —just another boring ceremony whose caps and gowns and pomp and circumstance were more irritating than thrilling, though he did feel great when it was all over. But to his grandparents, his father's parents, it was a big deal, something to be proud of, as they kept telling him. They came to stay for a week.

As usual, their visit meant a lot of fancy restaurants, a lot of shopping, and a lot of sitting around catching up on news of Al's hometown up north. But this time there was a difference. Despite his positive attitude, Al was clearly getting worse. He was losing weight, hair, energy. Dylan thought he looked ten years older. And though his grandparents didn't exactly dwell on Al's condition, they were definitely more subdued, more somber, than usual.

The subject of Al's death didn't crop up in conversation, except in ways Dylan found totally ridiculous.

Chapter Eleven

THE day after graduation, time suddenly expanded again, like a compressed spring snapping back to shape. Just like the songs said, school was out, surf was up, summer was here—that classic California summer Dylan had always loved. But this one wasn't starting out any too wonderfully. Barbra was off to saxophone lessons in L.A. three times a week, so she wasn't around much during the days. The hang glider still wasn't ready. And lying around on the beach, hanging ten on the board, and generally soaking up rays was just too mellow an existence to keep Dylan's mind from wandering down the June page of the calendar to the last day of the month.

His father's condition didn't help much, either. In his waking moments, he was still Smiling Al, brave and bold defier of death, but those waking moments were getting fewer and farther between. He was growing weaker and thinner almost by the day now, and with the painkillers he had to take just to get by, he was spending half his time in a horizontal position. He'd scheduled things perfectly, Dylan thought. In his condition, who could deny him the right to do what he was planning?

Kate made a stab at it at a family picnic Al had arranged. They were way up in the hills, looking out at the ridges below and the hot blue sky above, and the wine was disappearing, and everyone was easy and relaxed to the point where the whole scene was approaching the unreal perfection of some television commercial, and then Kate suddenly blurted out, "Al, can't you stay a little while longer?"

It wasn't the clearest question in the world, but Al got the meaning. He just lay back and stared up at the sky without answering.

"Things are going so well now," Kate said. "Couldn't you postpone it?"

Dylan expected Al to ask her why she thought things were going so well when he was in pain every second he was awake, but he just shook his head gently, almost imperceptibly.

"For a month or so? Please?" Kate begged.

"It's *why* things are going so well now," Al replied. "Don't spoil it."

Sighing, Kate walked off into the hills to be alone with her frustration. When she was out of earshot, Dylan posed a question of his own. "Don't you think you're being kind of selfish?"

Al kept staring up at the blue.

"Just asking," Dylan prodded.

Al exhaled, didn't turn his head. "Isn't it really selfish," he asked, "to try to cling to something you're going to have to give up anyway?"

This time Dylan didn't answer.

"That's what you and Kate want to do," Al went on. "Not me."

Al closed his eyes. He's the one who should've been on the debating team, Dylan thought. May as well let him sleep.

Dylan ambled into the hills, wishing there were something he could do for his father—something that would make him change his mind. Or even, failing that, something that would at least make his remaining days a little happier.

Something like the big testimonial dinner the department held a few days later to honor Al's retirement as a fireman. Dylan had been to such things before. He expected it to be another long affair with a lot of windy official speeches that didn't come close to capturing the bravery and valor they were supposed to be describing. But this time it was different. For one thing, Barbra was there beside him, and just about everybody who came over to the table to say hello to Al had some sort of compliment for her. And there was the poignancy of knowing that this testimonial dinner would be Al's last. Every firefighter who'd ever worked with or even heard about Al seemed to be there. As one of the speakers joked, if the hotel were ever going to decide to catch on fire, now would definitely be the time. In fact, a pumper and a hook-and-ladder were parked right out front in case some of the on-duty members of the department, wearing their uniforms at the tables, were called upon to make a hasty exit.

Considering the situation, the mood was more festive than Dylan had expected. Old friends and rookie firefighters alike came over to wish Al well, to tell him what a great example he was. Or to say what a shame it was about his early "retirement"—a word those firefighters, despite or maybe because of their intimacy with death, still used out of politeness and respect when they all knew exactly what they meant.

The talk around the dinner table was so animated that Dylan barely noticed what he was eating. Afterward the mayor went to the podium and recited a list of Al's achievements and awards since joining the force twenty years ago. When the fire commissioner spoke of Al's bravery under some of the worst possible conditions and Al's chief told about some of Al's most hair-raising rescues, Barbra looked as proud as if it were her father being honored.

But the speech everybody enjoyed the most was the one Marco D'Amato gave. Gruff, squat, earthy Marco, Al's oldest friend in the department, told story after story about their early days together. There was the time Al was so preoccupied with reading one of his philosophy books that he rushed to a fire without his pants. And then there was the time

Al had driven the pumper in precisely the wrong direction and, with typical Donaldson luck, was saved from disgrace when an even bigger fire happened to break out on that side of town. So the boys down at the firehouse had chipped in to buy Al a little memento of his service: a bronzed road map of the city of San Felipe.

Al went to the podium and accepted it with a couple of cracks about Marco's sleeping habits. Then the commissioner presented Al a plaque from all the members of the department. The mayor gave him a citation from the citizens of the city. Al was asked to say a few words.

He had done this so often that Dylan almost expected it to be routine, but this time Al's eyes filled up as he stared out at the sea of admirers. "I'm honored more than you know," he said, his voice thickening with emotion. "I have never seen so many friends in one place before. And I'd like to return your thanks. It's been a great job with great rewards, and it's been a great place to do it, and I want to thank you all for making my life so rich. You're really the ones who deserve the honors."

Applause rippled across the room, then boomed as everyone stood up. Dylan clapped until his hands hurt as the ovation went on and on. Finally the applause died down, and the mayor thanked everyone for coming, and there was another round of applause, and the well-wishers besieged Al once again.

When it was all over, Al slumped wearily in his chair and looked around the empty hall. "Quite an affair," he sighed, exhausted but deeply moved. Picking up the bronzed map, he smiled and shook his head. "That's Marco for you."

There was more Marco the next day at a party he'd arranged in his backyard, a barbecue for Al and his closest friends and their families. Barbra ran around with her camera, snapping every conceivable pose as the assembled throng got good and drunk on the keg beer. Halfway through the afternoon, Marco came up to Dylan and put his arm around him. "How you doing, kid?" he asked.

Dylan held up his cup of beer. "All right."

"Hey, I figured you'd do all right on that end. And that girl of yours—hell, every guy here's jealous. What I mean is, how are you holding up with your dad's—uh, you know."

Dylan knew, all right. He knew more than Marco did. "Okay." He shrugged. "It's not easy."

"Damn right it's not. Listen, if there's anything I can do—if you need help, money, if you just want an old fart's advice, whatever—I'm here. I just want you to know that. You can count on me. No shit, now."

Dylan was touched. When Marco said no shit, he meant it. Al had told dozens of stories about the things Marco had done for people. "I really appreciate it," Dylan said.

"Anytime." He leaned forward and spoke in a quieter, more urgent tone. "Seriously. Anytime. Before he goes or after."

Dylan nodded, and Marco moved back a little. "Still doing the hang gliding?"

"Not lately. Can't get the thing out of the shop."

"Oh, yeah, I heard about that. See, I told you that stuff was dangerous."

"Not at all. I got two scratches. Sometime I'll convince you to try it."

"Not me, pal. Fires are enough excitement for one lifetime."

Barbra sneaked up and snapped a picture of the two of them standing together. "All right, beautiful, let's have it," Marco said, reaching for the camera. "It's time we get a few of you." Barbra protested, refused, backed away, but Marco kept after her so persistently that she finally gave in. He posed her against the rose bushes, first without Dylan, then with.

The other adults at the party took a dutiful interest in Dylan, too, but with them he sensed that peculiar distance that somehow separates adults from kids, even though he was a high school graduate, a kid no longer. But if they were treating him like a kid, nobody was kidding him. One friend of his father's after another came up and said "Tough luck for your dad," or "Too bad about your father," or "It always happens to the good guys," in an awkward way. And Dylan would do the only thing he could think of, which was nod and agree, nod and agree.

The afternoon was warm, and Dylan was beginning to feel a little tipsy from the beer. As the shadows began creeping across the lawn and the light turned golden, Al climbed up on a chair and called for everyone's attention. "All right, people," he announced, "prepare yourself for the experience of a lifetime. Introducing the San Felipe Two!" He pointed to the house, from which Barbra made an impressive entrance, carrying her sax and his clarinet.

The crowd gathered around in a little circle to hear them play. Barbra gave Al a quizzical look, and he nodded back, and the two of them launched into a hot rendition of "Tiger Rag" that had people shouting "All right!" and "Go!" and "Do it!" Even with his untrained ears, Dylan could hear that their practice sessions had paid off. What excited Dylan most was the final number, Barbra's specialty, "Body and Soul," because of the way Barbra was looking at him, the way she was playing as if she were making love to him. For once, Dylan knew, he would be able to do something almost as special to return that love. But what still bothered him, gnawed at him, was that he wanted to do something even more special for his father. And he couldn't think of a thing.

The next day was Barbra's birthday, and Dylan had conjured up a whole headful of plans for it.

When he showed up at her door that evening, she greeted him in a summer dress so light and airy it looked as though it might blow away, the sort of romantic, frivolous dress he'd seen on models on magazine covers but never even heard of anybody actually wearing. But this time Dylan was almost her match, decked out in a linen sport coat his grandparents had bought him as a graduation present and—rarest of all things in his neighborhood—a tie.

"You look spectacular," he told her.

"So do you."

"Happy birthday!"

He handed her a package wrapped in pink tissue paper. "I can't possibly wait to open this," she said, giving him a kiss. The evening was beginning just the way Dylan had planned it. Except that as she led him inside, he sensed that she seemed different somehow. Something—something slight, her tone of voice, her smile, Dylan couldn't put his finger on it, but *something*—felt wrong.

They sat down on the couch. Dylan expectantly watched her undo the pink ribbon and unfold the paper. "From the hospital!" Barbra cried, throwing her arms around him. "You remembered!"

Of course he remembered. It was that big-eyed giraffe that had dangled over them on the day they'd met. But why did Barbra suddenly seem so . . . what? . . . strange? "He wanted to live with you," Dylan joked, trying not to let things throw him. Maybe it was just Al's suicide making *him* weird. "Told me so himself."

"He goes right onto my pillow. Whenever I look at him, I'll think of you."

"Come on. I'm better-looking than that."

"Don't flatter yourself," Barbra said with a smile. They exchanged more kisses for a while—why did she seem so restrained?—and then Dylan looked at his watch and realized they'd better be heading for dinner. Barbra gave him one last peck and abruptly grabbed her purse.

The evening could not have been more perfect. As they drove up the coast, the sun headed downward into layers of clouds that turned electric orange, then deep red. As they parked at the restaurant, the sky began to glow a muted purple. "Even the sun is celebrating," Dylan said softly, and he saw a shiver of delight run across Barbra's shoulders.

The restaurant was a fancy French place he'd been to only once before, with his grandparents. Dylan felt a little silly in his coat and tie, but when the waiter didn't bother carding him or even raising an eyebrow when he ordered two glasses of white wine, he realized a coat and tie could conceivably have their purposes. He toasted Barbra's birthday and her beauty, and they clinked glasses just like in the movies. Staring out at the crashing waves and the deepening purple of the twilight, they were mesmerized by the magnificence of the coast. "You can't see a sunset over the Atlantic," Dylan remarked.

"Sure you can," Barbra told him. "You see it reflected in the windows of the boats in the harbor. Or over Long Island Sound."

Dylan frowned. "Another belief shattered."

"Come on, Dylan," Barbra said, her smile glowing in the candlelight. "You don't have to sell me on California. This is the most beautiful birthday sunset ever."

The dinner was beautiful, too. The waiter was friendly, patiently translating the few French dishes Barbra hadn't heard of, helpfully offering suggestions, politely refusing to wince (as Barbra did) at Dylan's fractured French. "Back East," Barbra said, "if you and I went to a place like this alone, they'd treat us like two little kids who didn't belong. Here they really seem to want to make sure we're enjoying ourselves."

Which they were. The food was wonderful, from the watercress soup, to the snails in garlic butter that Barbra insisted Dylan try, to the thin slices of veal in an intense, rich brown sauce. The French Bordeaux was eight years old—bottled, as Barbra pointed out, when they both were still in grade school. For dessert they had a pastry called croquembouche, pieces of a huge tower made of little puffs covered with caramel sauce. As they lingered over their coffee, the dark enveloped the coast in shades of indigo, the moon added highlights of silver, and Dylan felt more adult than he ever had in his life.

Barbra put her hand on his. "Thank you," she told him, her eyes filled with joy. "It's been a beautiful evening."

"And it's not over yet," Dylan replied, his heart trying to soar but somehow held back by a vague gust of coolness he sensed from Barbra. It must just be me, he told himself. Quit worrying about Al and pay attention to Barbra.

Fog was rolling in gently as they returned to the car. "You drive," Barbra said, and Dylan agreed. But they didn't drive anywhere right away, holding each other close in the car for a long while before they hit the road.

The wine—the whole experience—had gone to Dylan's head, but he was sober enough to be careful in the fog that was so much a part of life along the coast. When they pulled into Barbra's driveway, he leaned forward and kissed her again. "There's something for you in the Blazer," he murmured.

Her eyes lit up once more. They walked to the truck with their hands around each other's waists. Dylan opened the tailgate and took out a huge, flat, floppy package swathed in pink crepe paper. "What in the world is that?" Barbra asked.

Dylan shrugged coyly. "Take it inside and find out."

He held it for her as she fumbled with the locks, and when they got to the living room, he laid it on the coffee table. "I can't even begin to imagine what this is," Barbra said as she began unwrapping it. What revealed itself beneath the paper was a strangely shaped posterboard. Pink. The shape turned out to be a heart, a heart fifty sizes too big for any known beast. On it, Dylan had drawn the enormous words "I LOVE YOU," and in normal-sized letters at the bottom, he'd signed "Happy Birthday. Dylan."

Barbra threw her arms around him. "It's wonderful, Dyl. You're a hopeless romantic!"

Dylan wondered about her word choice. "Hopeless?"

"Hopeless!" Barbra repeated happily, hugging him tighter.

"Barbra, is that you?" a thick voice half shouted, half mumbled from down the hall.

Barbra drew away from Dylan and sat up. "Yeah, it's me."

"Okay," the voice said, and went silent again. Her father. Dylan had met him a couple of times. A businessman. Wore suits. Usually smelled of alcohol.

"Drunk again," Barbra pouted. "Didn't even remember my birthday."

So *that* was it. She really *was* upset. "Come on. Forget it."

"I can't," she said, shaking her head, losing the cool that she had carried with her all evening. "It hurts too much. God, if only he were like Al."

She picked up Dylan's monster birthday card and stared at it as tears welled up in her eyes. "Oh, I'll live," she said determinedly. "You make me so happy, Dylan." She pulled him close and cried into his shoulder.

You'll live, Dylan thought bitterly, stroking her hair, but there's somebody else who won't. If you think it hurts now, just wait till Saturday.

He held it for her as she fumbled with the lock and when they got to the living room, he laid it on the coffee table. "I can't even begin to imagine what it is," Barbra said as she began unwrapping it revealed itself to be the paper was at

Chapter Twelve

"**W**ELL, gang," Al Said, dumping a file folder of documents onto the dining room table, "let's get the busy work out of the way so we can party." What that meant was that he and Dylan and Kate were about to discuss the minor details, the boring logistics, of Life Without Father.

"I guess the first thing we should do is go over the will." Al took a folded sheet of paper out of an envelope that was yellow at the edges. "I've talked this over with Matthias"—Matthias was their lawyer—"and he says it's still okay. Incidentally, Kate, he should be just about the first person you contact after I'm gone."

"Of course," Kate said, annoyed at being told something she already knew all too well.

"Can I have a look?" Dylan asked.

"That's what we're here for," Al replied, handing him the page.

It was one sheet, only one, signed by his father and three witnesses—Marco and his ex-wife (back then, they were still married), and a fireman named Bjornstrand that Dylan dimly remembered as having retired a few years ago. What the will said, basically, was that everything Al owned would go to Kate, and if they both should die at the same time, everything would go to Dylan. What impressed Dylan about it, for a legal document, was its simplicity —a lot less complicated than, say, the warranty on his glider. He was surprised at how straightforward and direct the will was, how easily you could express your wishes for what was to happen after you no longer existed. Death might not be so complicated after all.

"Any questions?" Al asked as Dylan put the sheet back on the table.

"Seems simple enough."

"That's what I said when Matthias drew it up. But you know lawyers. He said it's not as simple as you might think. And if you're really rich, apparently it can get to be pretty damned complicated. Anyway, that's one thing we don't have to worry about."

He thrust the will toward Kate, and she pushed it back. "I know what's in it," she said. "It's exactly the same as mine."

"Okay." Al folded up the will and put it back in the envelope. He took some thicker documents from the pile. "Let's see. Here's the life insurance policy from the city, and here's our own policy."

Dylan glanced at them. Now this was more what he expected—page after page of fine-print legal confusion about benefits and annuities and exclusions and limitations and beneficiaries and the deceased. A weird thought suddenly crossed his mind. "Uh, I hate to bring this up," he blurted out, "but do these cover death by suicide?"

"Dylan!" Kate scolded.

"Fair question," Al said. "I checked it out myself, as a matter of fact. The answer's yes. They don't cover it for the first couple of years, so people can't just go out and buy a whole lot of insurance and then kill themselves the next day so their survivors can collect. These policies have been in force long enough so that I'm covered."

"Well, hooray," Kate sneered.

"Hooray is right," Al said. "At least give me some credit. I wouldn't've even considered this if I'd thought it'd leave you unprotected."

"Many thanks," Kate muttered.

"Okay. There's also money due from my pension fund. You have to go down to city hall and fill out some forms to get it. As far as health insurance goes, Kate, your policy from school will cover you both, but it expires for Dylan on his twentieth birthday. So remember to check up on that when the time comes, Dyl. Stanford's student health can probably help you out."

He pawed through the rest of the pile. "Now, Kate, here are the records for all the credit cards and bank accounts and car title and insurance and so on—stuff that's in both our names. I've been phoning around finding out what to do about them, and it's all down here on this sheet. Except for one or two items, basically it's just a matter of notifying somebody and sending back the credit card that has my name on it."

As Al continued through the pile, Dylan tuned out and only half listened to what he was saying. He was admiring Al's calm, methodical way of handling things, of anticipating every possibility. Dylan remembered how one of the guys down at the firehouse had told him how great Al was at knowing beforehand exactly what was likely to happen in all sorts of circumstances. It meant that under pressure he could size up a situation fast and decide what to do about it. It was that careful preplanning, along with Al's amazing instincts, that had helped keep him alive through all those years as a firefighter. Now, Dylan thought with both bitterness and admiration, it was going to help him die.

"About the funeral," Al was saying. "Basically, just as it says in the will, I don't want one, no ceremony, and I haven't changed my mind. We've been members of that funeral society for a long time, so once you get the death certificate, all you have to do is phone them. They'll take me out and set up a cremation."

Cremation. Dylan shivered. Details, details. Death wasn't so simple after all. Dylan could see from the look on Kate's face that her patience was wearing thin, but she didn't say a word. "No flowers," Al went on. "If people want to memorialize me, they can send donations to the firefighters' survivors' fund, which it also says in the will."

"I guess that's pretty much it," he said, stacking up the papers. "Oh, yeah, we have to go to the bank tomorrow and get the safe deposit box changed to your name only, Kate. If you have a joint box, they seal it up when either person dies. Some sort of legal thing I found out about. Anyway, that's the one major item left to take care of now. The rest is all down here, and it can wait. Any questions?"

"Just one," Kate snapped.

"I think you know the answer to that one already, Kate," Al said. He gathered up the documents.

That was Tuesday night. Wednesday morning, Dylan got word from the shop that the glider was ready. Kate happened to overhear him on the phone, and the minute he hung up, she threw a minor fit. How could he even think about getting the glider right now? Didn't he understand the situation?

Dylan was in no mood to argue. He went out the door, got into the Blazer, and headed down the coast. He couldn't wait to be reunited with that glider. When he saw it in the shop, it gave him the usual thrill. Though paying for the repairs stung hard, he was overjoyed to have his wings back.

The repairman told him the glider had already been flight-tested, but he urged Dylan to try it at the beach, close to the ground, before taking it up high again. Sometimes, the guy said, the flight characteristics changed a little after a repair, and it was a good idea to find out about it fifteen feet up instead of fifteen hundred. Besides, he added slyly, "from the look of that strut when you came in here, you may have been outflying your ability just the least little bit."

Dylan took the hint. But at that hour of the day that time of year, the beach would be swarming with people. Dylan had to wait until early—very early—the next morning to make his test flight. Alone on the dunes in the first light of morning, he set up the glider, made his safety checks, strapped himself in, and made a low pass across the sand and the beer cans and paper cups left over from the day before. It felt glorious. The glider performed perfectly. He went up again. And in the air he suddenly realized what he wanted to do more than anything.

Back home, he stormed through the front door and into the kitchen. "How you feeling?" he asked Al.

Al looked up from his coffee and shrugged. "No more rotten than usual. Glider okay?"

Dylan grabbed him by the arm. "Come on. Bring your pills and whatever else you need."

"What?"

"Come on. I want you to come see me fly."

Al stood up, dumbfounded. Then Kate came into the room. "No," she said, firm as a rock.

Dylan and Al glanced at her as she stood there in the doorway, cold with indignation. Then they looked at each other. "I've got to get a couple of things," Al said, hurrying upstairs to the bathroom for his pills.

Kate was livid. "Dylan, you can't do this!"

"He's not going to fly," Dylan said calmly. "He's just going to watch."

"He's not even in shape to drive."

"I'll get Jay or Sean or somebody to drive."

"Dylan, don't you have any respect for me?"

"It doesn't have anything to do with respect for you. I've been wanting to do something special for Dad for the last two months now. But I couldn't see giving him a present—I mean, really, what's the point?—and I didn't know what else to do. I'd like to fly for him, that's all."

Kate glowered at him.

"Look, just once. I promise. No showing off. Just once so he can see me do it before he dies."

"Maybe he's not going to die," Kate said. Dylan stood and stared, realizing once more how hard this all was for her.

Al came down the stairs. "Ready?" he asked.

"If you are," Dylan said, holding the door open. Al went outside.

"Damn it, wait for me," Kate said as Dylan stepped out the door. "I may as well see this, too."

So in this crazy way, Dylan thought as they drove up into the mountains, they were all together again, just like old times, Dylan and Kate and Al in the front seat of the Blazer, thanks to that beautiful wing behind them. It was still early, too early even for gliding fanatics to be up yet now that they had whole long summer days for their flying, so Dylan had to stop at the clearing to set up the streamers.

From the ledge, Dylan described his flight plan. "Hell of a long way down," Al noted as he looked out over the valley. Kate, skittish, stayed half a dozen steps back from the edge. She didn't say a word.

Dylan took the glider out of the truck, and he waved to his parents as they drove off with shouts of "Good trip!" and "Be careful!" Then he began setting up the wing, fighting back tears that for no apparent reason seemed to push into his eye sockets, trying to obey the broken record in the back of his head that seemed to keep saying "Don't screw up!" over and over again. When he finished all the safety checks, he turned the glider sideways to the wind, made his way to the edge, and looked down. There in the distance was the Blazer, and, leaning against it, there were his parents, tiny figures, looking up, waiting.

He walked back from the edge, pointed the sail into the wind, and took a deep breath.

Just once.

I promise.

Don't screw up.

Go!

He ran. He jumped. He flew. He spotted a thermal, caught it, rose with it. He floated down, found another thermal, soared again. His heart soared too, somehow sucking those tears back into their ducts. He descended slowly, gently. Near the ground, he caught sight of his parents, flashed them a wide, heartfelt grin. Then, all business, he skimmed over the fluttering streamers and touched down perfectly —ready for another flight.

Just once. I promised.

Al was whooping and hollering, cheering Dylan's graceful landing, and even Kate had a smile on her face. "Incredible!" Al said, slapping Dylan on the back. "Not so bad, huh, Kate?"

"Not bad at all," she agreed.

"Thanks, Dylan," Al said, exuberant. "Now I know why you're such a nut about this."

"I'm glad I saw it, Dylan," Kate said, calm and relaxed as he began dismantling the glider, "but I wouldn't do that for all the gold in Fort Knox."

Dylan drove home in glory, his parents suddenly full of questions about what it was like, how you could actually go up when gravity was pulling you down, how you changed directions in the air. Dylan answered patiently and knowledgeably. When they got home, he even set up the glider in the driveway to help him with his explanations.

Al was trying on the harness when Barbra drove up. "Don't tell me you're going to fly!" she joked.

"Not even off the roof," Al replied, undoing the straps.

Dylan eased the sail to the driveway and gave Barbra a kiss. "Enough of that," Al said, a slight touch of fatigue in his voice. "We've got some jazz to do."

"Right," Barbra said, following him inside. "When you get done, Dylan, come be our audience."

Dylan didn't have the guts to. As he dismantled the glider, he could hear the music coming from the den. Al was playing his heart out—better than any amateur had a right to, as Barbra remarked afterward. But unless Al suddenly changed his plans for Saturday, it was going to be the last time he and Barbra would ever see each other. Everybody was in on the secret but her.

As usual, Al kept his poker face. Barbra stayed for lunch, but the talk was all light and fluffy, how good-looking her saxophone teacher was, how one of his other students had a bumper sticker that said "The Joy of Sax," how many good jazz musicians there were down in L.A. When Dylan and Barbra took off for the beach, he couldn't believe that Al would just let her go without at least a big hug or some sort of special farewell. But no. Al just said good-bye and that was it. He didn't even flinch when Barbra said "See you." It pissed Dylan off so much he nearly told her about Al's plans. But he didn't.

"At least you didn't tell her to practice up for next time," Dylan chided Al that evening.

"I can't spread the news all over town, Dylan. If I'd acted differently, she might've gotten suspicious. Believe me, it's better this way."

"Then why'd you have to tell us? Mom and me."

Al shook his head. "Aren't you glad you had the chance to show me that gliding this morning? I sure am. Maybe if you didn't know how long I was going to be here, you'd never have gotten around to it." Zapped again, Dylan thought. Not knowing what to say, he just walked away. Al seemed to have his life planned down to the last second.

The big event for Friday—Al's last full day alive, if everything went according to plan—was an outing and picnic way up in the hills along with Marco and a few other family friends. Dylan had invited Barbra, of course, but she'd declined. He tried again on the phone that evening.

"I told you, I can't," she said. "Sax lesson."

"Play hooky," Dylan suggested.

"Come on, Dylan. Lay off."

"It'll be like that afternoon at Marco's. You and Al can play duets for us."

"I'd love to, Dylan, but my lessons come first."

Something wrong again? Dylan detected just a touch of desperation in his voice as he said "Please?"

"Come on, Dylan, don't push me. I need some time to myself. I can't spend every minute with you and your family."

Every minute? Lately it seemed they'd hardly been spending any time together. Dylan half considered betraying his father and telling her just *why* he needed her support so badly, why he wanted her to be with him at that picnic, but he let the subject drop. Barbra went to her saxophone lesson.

It was just as well. At the picnic, Dylan could see that Al intended to keep things light right up to the end: no wallowing in self-pity, no morbid displays of emotion, just a nice, pleasant day with friends and food and beer. True, there was more reminiscing than usual—stories about the time Al had done this or Marco had done that or Cesar had done the other thing, but it felt easy and comfortable, and Dylan was included in it. They told embarrassing stories about when Dylan was little and spilled a glass of milk all over the fire commissioner's brand-new suit, and the time Dylan locked himself in the men's room at the firehouse but somehow managed to get it open just before one of the rookies chopped the door down with an ax.

Dylan was tempted to tell some stories of his own, but he was comfortably high on his beer, feeling so elated, so isolated from the world and so glad of it, that he kept knocking down cans of Olympia to keep the blissful mood, to avoid confronting the sadness right below the surface. As they were clearing away

117

the blankets and the trash, the beer took its revenge. Dylan went down on his knees and puked what seemed an underground river of foul-tasting slime. Through the throbbing in his head, he could see Marco and Al looking at him with a mixture of tenderness, amusement, and disgust, and the thought came to him that if he needed first aid, at least there were people around who knew something about it, and then he puked again and lay back in the Honda's reclining front seat, and somehow or other he vaguely perceived himself being helped up the stairs and falling into bed in an absolute stupor.

Chapter Thirteen

"COME on, get up," Kate was saying softly, poking Dylan gently in the arm. He opened his eyes and quickly shut them again. His head felt as though it had grown fungus inside. "Come on, Dylan. We're having a special breakfast."

Breakfast? He winced at the thought. "Please, Dylan," Kate begged. "Before it gets cold."

He nodded, and she went out the door. He dragged himself out of bed. She hadn't said a word about the fact that he was still in his street clothes from the day before, street clothes lightly flecked with dried vomit. He decided it'd be a good idea to at least change his shirt. He went into the bathroom and splashed cold water on his face. Then he shuffled downstairs, still in a daze of fatigue and hangover. When he saw his father at the table, he remembered what all the fuss was about, the special breakfast and everything. Suddenly his throat tightened up, and he almost felt like puking again.

"How you feeling?" Al asked him as he sat down.

Dylan shrugged. He couldn't face his father. He felt embarrassed and ashamed, mostly about getting drunk and spoiling his father's last full day alive, but it was more than just that. He felt that if he looked at Al, he'd simply burst into tears.

Kate set the carafe of coffee on the table and went into the kitchen to get the waffles. Dylan could smell them. Waffles with ice cream and maple syrup were a traditional breakfast treat in the family. They were special, ridiculously rich and fattening, something reserved for only two or three occasions a year. Dylan looked at his orange juice and coffee and wondered how he'd manage to force them down—let alone the ice-cream-topped waffle Kate was setting in front of him.

"Remember the first time you had these?" Al reminisced. Dylan just stared at his plate.

"Probably not," Al went on. "You must've been about three. I remember you picked up the ice cream and threw it at the wall. Kate asked why, and you said, very firmly, 'Ice cream is for dessert, and you don't get dessert at breakfast time.'"

Dylan forced a smile, but he still couldn't meet his father's eyes. His own eyes were filming over. He reached for the orange juice and took a gulp, but it felt raw, acidic going down. He tried the coffee, found it a little more soothing. But he had absolutely no appetite. He forced down a sliver of ice cream. The coolness felt good on his throat, but it seemed to bore a hole in his stomach.

Al was wolfing down his waffle. Emotion certainly hadn't spoiled his appetite. Nor his attitude of good cheer. "I really appreciate these, Kate," he said with his mouth full. "The first time I ever had these was when you made them for me back in Berkeley, remember?"

Kate remembered, all right. Dylan could see it in the way she nibbled on her lower lip as she nodded. If all the tears that were welling up around here burst through their dams right now, Dylan thought, the whole damned room would flood out. It was around nine o'clock, he guessed. His father had decided to kill himself at high noon. How could they possibly keep this up till then?

He poked at his food in silence. Al got up and went into the kitchen for a second helping. Dylan looked at Kate. "Pretend," she whispered.

That said it all. Pretend he was hungry. Pretend Al would change his mind. Pretend.

"Anybody else?" Al asked, gesturing with his plate. Looking away, Dylan and Kate shook their heads.

"Sure, now?" Al asked. Dylan and Kate silently nodded.

"All the more for me," Al said like an overgrown school kid. He went back into the kitchen and returned with an even bigger plateful. Maybe he's given up on the sleeping pills, Dylan thought sardonically. Maybe he's going to do it with an overdose of maple syrup.

"I'm going to go wash up," Dylan announced, pushing himself away from the table. He took his mother's plate and his own, scraped them, and stuck them in the dishwasher. Then he locked himself in the bathroom.

He hoped he could prolong his time in there as much as possible, so he wouldn't have to face any more of this horrible morning than was absolutely necessary. As he sat on the toilet, he tried to concentrate on an article in the movie section of a copy of *Newsweek* someone had left there, but his mind was thick, fuzzy, unable to focus. He gave up and went to the sink to shave.

He stared at his face in the mirror. What made it alive? What kept it from being dead? The blood coursing through his veins? The will to live, housed somewhere up there in his brain cells? The genetic programming that somehow kept his body going on a sort of automatic pilot?

He lathered his face and picked up the razor. It was the latest model, a swivel-head job with the twin blades safely shielded in plastic, but it somehow reminded him of all the films he'd seen in which people used straight razors to kill each other. He remembered a discussion from media class about how they did that special effect that let you see the blood spurt out as the razor slashed open the skin, something he'd seen probably fifty times by now, especially during his horror-movie period. His classmates found the effect almost funny, but it always made him squirm. He wondered . . .

Hell! His hand slipped, and the blood bubbled up on his face in that neat round blob it always made. He ripped off a piece of toilet paper and stuck it to the cut. It stung a little. Pain. Was that what living meant?

He finished shaving, splashed cold water on his face, and delicately lifted the pinkish paper from his cut. It blobbed up again. Persistent, damn it. He found the box of Band-Aids in the medicine cabinet, took out a little round one, and stuck it neatly over the wound. Battle scar. Beautiful.

He lingered in the shower until his fingertips began to wrinkle. When he finished brushing and flossing his teeth, there was nothing left to do but go downstairs. He hoped his parents—his father, anyway—would still be in their bedroom, using their bathroom to wash up, get dressed, whatever. His nausea had gone, but he still wasn't ready to face them.

Dylan sat down on the living room couch and leafed through a copy of *California*. Anything to pass the time. He felt the way he did when he was waiting for his parents to get ready for a vacation trip, having to hang around with nothing to do until they were ready to go. Except now he was waiting for something he didn't want to happen, something he wasn't looking forward to the least bit, something he dreaded.

He wondered what his parents were talking about in the bedroom. If they were talking. What could you talk about at a time like this? Was Al telling Kate how much he loved her and Kate saying the same thing back? Or were they arguing, his mother telling his father to wait, begging him to live until his natural death, bargaining for another month, another week, another day? Dylan thought about going to the door and listening in, as he'd done on rare occasions when he'd felt it absolutely urgent to find out what his parents were saying about him when they thought he wasn't listening, but he remembered how dirty it always made him feel. Give them their privacy, he decided. It's just about the only thing they have left.

Then Kate came down the stairs with a look of resignation on her face, and Al followed right behind, carrying the family photo albums. Creative suicide, all right, Dylan thought bitterly. He's going to make us go through this with him every step of the way. Dylan hoped he could keep from spoiling it. And wished he could spoil it completely.

Al sat down on the couch between Dylan and Kate, spread the books out on the coffee table, and opened the oldest one. "Here I am at the ripe old age of a day or two," he said, his humor a little forced, a little strained. As he slowly paged through the books, Al told the anecdotes they'd laughed at dozens of times before. But Kate and Dylan held back at first, unable to bear the emotional weight. Al sensed it and began drawing them out, forcing them to participate in his last review of these memories.

"Remember this?" he would ask, pointing to a shot of Dylan with Mickey Mouse at Disneyland, and Kate would recall how much six-year-old Dylan had fussed when that picture had been snapped, and Dylan would protest that there'd been a very good reason—Goofy had bumped into his cotton candy and knocked it out of his hand. And there'd be laughter in the living room just like in the old days, and Al would keep it flowing with another story from the past, usually one they didn't even have a picture of. Dylan suddenly realized that the snapshots were only vague reminders of all that had really been happening back

123

when they were taken. There were no pictures of the first time he'd picked up a lizard in the backyard or the time he'd fallen into a fish pond at a museum in Pasadena, yet those memories were far more vivid to him than the birthday parties and grade school ceremonies in the photos.

The memories were flooding in now, every bit as intensely as in the commercials for cameras and film. Time was flying in every direction. Before he knew it, it was eleven-thirty. Al interrupted himself in mid-laugh, said, "Listen, I have to go to the john," and excused himself.

A jolt of pure terror shot through Dylan's heart. Al's departure was his way of changing the tone of the moment. Dylan looked at Kate. Her cheeks were trembling. The terror had hit her too.

Chapter Fourteen

"CAN I see you for a couple of minutes, Dylan?" Al called.

Dylan glanced at Kate, and she looked back at him as if to say "Go on." Dylan hesitantly climbed the short flight of stairs to the second floor and followed his father into the big bedroom.

It was immaculate for a change. Dylan noticed that the bed had been made neatly, the flowered spread tidily tucked back under the front of the pillows in a way that his parents rarely bothered with. The dresser and night table were clear of the heating pads and drugs and cosmetics and dirty laundry that usually cluttered them. It wasn't that his parents were normally slobs, just that they were usually too busy with other things to keep cleaning the place up every fifteen seconds. But they'd certainly cleaned it up now, as though they were expecting company. Which, of course, they were.

Al sat down at the foot of the bed and motioned for Dylan to sit across from him on the chair. Usually it had a pair of pants or a belt or something on it, but now it was totally clear. Dylan sat down awkwardly.

"Well, I've made all my plans," Al said, gesturing nervously with his hands, "but now I don't know how to begin this."

Dylan hesitated, then spoke his mind. "You don't have to."

"Dylan," Al pleaded, "don't make it harder than it already is."

Why not? Dylan kept thinking to himself. He's not

that sick yet. His pain can't be that bad. Why *not* make it hard for him to do this? But all Dylan said was, "Sorry."

"I mean, now that we're here, I don't know exactly how to say good-bye," Al went on. "I want this to be a little better than the usual 'take care of your mother' lecture before I went off to a convention. This time it's for keeps."

A small shiver ran up Dylan's spine.

"I wasn't sure whether I should talk to you first or your mother, but I decided on doing it this way. Anyway, we can all be together right at the end."

Dylan recognized his father's pain, both the physical agony of his illness and the emotional torture of the moment, in the slumped way he was sitting, the way his hands clasped and unclasped uncertainly. "What I want to say, first of all," Al continued, "is that I love you more than I think you know."

"I do know," Dylan said as the shivers grew icier.

"Then I'm proud that you do. And I want you to realize I'm not doing this thing for any reason you or your mother should feel the least bit guilty about after it's all over. I've tried to explain it before, and I hope you understand it by now. But if you don't, if there's any question in your mind, I want you to ask me. I want you to understand."

"I understand it," Dylan said, even though inside his head his brain cells were hollering "Why? Why?"

"You sure?" Al asked.

"I understand it," Dylan said. "I don't have to like it."

Al shrugged. "If you really understood, I think you would like it. Or at least respect it. I've done my best to keep things cheerful, to spread some joy the last couple of months. I think you realize how difficult this is for me, how tough a choice it is."

He looked up, and their eyes met. "Please don't do this, Dad! Please!" Dylan nearly blurted out, but he

126

let the words rattle around in his head until they died out.

"I'm trying to avoid all the old clichés," Al said. "I mean, I don't want to say 'you're the man of the house now,' even though you are. And I don't even want to tell you you're a man now, that you're grown up. I think you know that already, and if you don't, my telling you won't make you believe it. Same reason I'm not going to sum up all the things we've tried to teach you over the years, because whatever I say in the next few minutes won't make up for eighteen years. Besides, if you want to know the truth, I think you've learned your lessons pretty damned well."

"Thanks," Dylan said softly. In the silence that followed, he could hear his parents' little alarm clock ticking off the precious seconds one by one.

Al stared at him. "I guess what I really want to say is, don't let this throw you. One of the things it takes a long time to learn is how much of life is luck—good, bad, in-between. Sometimes you can help make your luck. But you'd be surprised how often you can't. When I think back to when I was your age—hell, how I hate that phrase, 'When I was your age,' excuse me —anyway, back then I had no idea I'd wind up doing what I do for a living or marrying a woman like your mom, or having a kid who'd know how to jump off cliffs and live to tell about it. I can't even remember exactly what I expected, but it sure wasn't anything like what I got. What I got was a lot better. I was lucky. You've been, too, so far, at least the way I see it. I've been lucky to be able to watch you grow up. I guess what I'm telling you is that you're not going to have that luck all the time. If your luck turns bad for a while, ride it out. It can turn back again."

Maybe it isn't too late, Dylan thought. Maybe he's trying to tell me something. "Isn't that what you're doing? Refusing to ride out your luck?" Dylan demanded. "Those miracles happen. Your luck could change."

Al sighed, ran his fingers through what was left of his hair. "You're smart, Dylan. You see right through me. You're absolutely right, from your point of view. From here, it's just a question of accelerating my fate a little. My luck's run out."

"You can't know that."

Al looked into his lap, then stared straight at Dylan with eyes that looked terribly old. "I do."

They looked at each other for what seemed a small lifetime. "I have something to say to you now," Dylan finally spoke, trying to hold back his tears, trying to match his father's bravery, if bravery was what it was. "I'm very proud of you. I have been since I was a little kid. I wish I could repay you for everything somehow."

Al stood up. "Mind if I hug you?"

Dylan rose, and they held each other tight, and tears fell heavily from four eyes at once. They wore out six Kleenexes wiping their cheeks. Finally Al sat down and folded his hands again and said, "Ask your mother to come up."

Dylan left hesitantly, looking back at his father sitting there alone on the bed. When he got to the living room, he found his mother on the couch, staring at the coffee table, as though she hadn't moved a muscle since he'd left. "He wants to see you," Dylan said quietly. Kate pushed herself up from the couch and trudged up the stairs.

Alone in the living room, Dylan mentally took stock of his surroundings. Almost everything had a story, damn it—the bookshelves he'd "helped" Al build when he was about six, the sofa he and Kate had picked out after endless evenings cruising furniture stores, the old chair Al refused to get rid of even though it puffed out stuffing every time someone sat on it. Even the picture album itself had its story. He remembered how much trouble he had picking it out for his parents' wedding anniversary a few years back.

What were they talking about now? He wondered if they were making love, then thought no, this was too sad a time to make love. Probably they were simply exchanging the same sorts of painful, difficult words he and his father had just spoken, and probably they would end up tearfully holding each other the way he and his father had.

There was no clock ticking in the living room. Outside, the day was typical summer gorgeous, the kind of day when normally he'd be out at the beach or up at the ledge or hiking through the woods with Barbra. Through the glass patio doors, he could see the bird feeder his father had made and the chaise longues reflecting the sunlight. That light streamed through the door at a steep angle, leading his eye to the living room end of the table, where his father always sat at meals so he could make a quick exit in case he was called to a fire. Dylan shuddered at the realization that his father would never again be sitting in that chair. Or the one in the living room. Or . . .

"Dylan?" Al called in a choked voice.

Dylan made his way up the stairs slowly, as if he were going to his execution. Which, in a way, he was. A part of him, he was sure, would die in there with Al. Moist-eyed, his father and mother gathered him up into one last desperate communal hug, and his own tears flowed again as he pressed against them. This was it, he knew. No handshakes, no words would come after. He squeezed his father as hard as he could for as long as he could.

The circle broke apart. Al drew Dylan to him one last time, and then Dylan watched his parents' final embrace. "It's time," Al murmured. As Kate and Dylan stood in the hallway, Al nodded good-bye to them, went into the bedroom, and quickly shut the door.

Dylan and Kate glanced at each other, surprised to

find that neither one of them was breaking down again. They somehow found the strength to do what they were supposed to: go downstairs and wait. Al would be taking all those barbiturates he'd cleverly hoarded over the past months—toss and gulp, toss and gulp, toss and gulp—and then he would lie down on that neatly made bed and wait for the drugs to work. Dylan and Kate were supposed to wait exactly one hour, then go up and check his pulse. By then, there wasn't supposed to be any pulse. Dylan or Kate would call the ambulance, and the whole thing would be over.

Or would it? What if the pills didn't work? What if something else went wrong? What if—the question kept gnawing away at Dylan—what if he or Kate phoned the ambulance *right now?*

They could pump out your stomach at the hospital, Dylan knew. Even if the stuff had gotten into your system, they could probably revive you with other drugs and you could live to tell about it. All it would take was one phone call.

Dylan was glad he couldn't see the phone from where he was sitting on the couch. He wasn't glad he could see Kate. Biting her lower lip, twisting up her face, she looked tortured, desperate. She was probably thinking the same things he was. How could they just sit there and let Al do this? How could they just sit there and let a human being, one they loved deeply, take his life?

But what would happen if they saved him? Would he thank them? More likely he'd just be angry, stubborn, determined to finish what he'd started and do it quick and get it over with, without any warning, without any tenderness. Still, he *might* thank them. He just might. Going that close to the brink might change his head. And he wouldn't be able to do anything—thank them *or* get angry with them—once he was dead. If they were going to stop him, they'd have to act fast.

But Dylan didn't act. He didn't move. Al had planned this, explained it, asked for support. Dylan and Kate had done their best to get him to back out, but he'd gone through with it. It was what he wanted, or what he said he wanted. Besides, he was in pain, probably a lot worse pain than he admitted. Besides, no matter what happened, he'd be dead soon enough.

The argument raged on in Dylan's head. He could see Al take the pills, lie back on the bed, shut his eyes, wait for the end. He could hear Al's instructions: wait a full hour, check my pulse, and whatever you do, don't phone the ambulance early.

Did life drain out of you, Dylan wondered, or did it suddenly end, boom, one minute you're alive, the next you're dead? Or did it somehow depend on the circumstances? What about all those people who'd supposedly "died" and then were brought back to life?

He looked at his mother. Her eyes were closed, her face contorted with sadness and pain. She was trying to relax, Dylan could see, trying to summon up some fragment of inner peace. And not being any more successful at it than he was. Overwhelmed, Dylan slouched back, shut his own eyes, and tried to clear his mind.

The stillness was maddening. Dylan could hear his mother breathing. The refrigerator humming. Birds chirping. Cars rumbling in the distance. Life going on, Dylan thought. Life going on.

The phone rang.

Dylan's eyes sprang open. Kate looked at him. He certainly didn't want to answer the phone. What could he possibly say to anyone at a moment like this? Yet it kept on, insistent, and Dylan realized it would be ringing in the bedroom, too, disturbing his father, if his father wasn't already beyond disturbing. He went to the kitchen, picked up the receiver, and put it to his ear without saying a word.

There was silence on the other end, then a surprised "Hello?"

Barbra. Of all the people Dylan did not want to speak with at that instant. "Hello," he muttered thickly.

"Are you okay?"

"Yeah," he grunted, wondering what she meant.

"You didn't say anything at first."

"Yeah."

"Listen, I know we weren't supposed to get together tonight, but I changed my plans. There's something I want to talk to you about."

"I'm, uh, busy right now," he struggled to say, trying to keep his voice low so Kate wouldn't hear.

"Are you all right? Something sounds wrong."

If you only knew, Dylan thought. "I've got to go. We'll talk later, okay?"

"Really, Dylan, is something wrong?"

"We'll talk. 'Bye."

He hung up. Then, knowing Barbra, he realized she would probably call right back, try to find out what the problem was. He lifted the phone off the hook, lay the receiver on the kitchen table, and went back to the living room. "Barbra?" his mother asked.

Dylan nodded, and Kate winced and closed her eyes again. As he slumped down on the couch, the phone gave off a loud "reminder" noise that sounded like a siren.

Dylan jumped up and went back to the kitchen. He didn't want to hang up the phone; he had half a mind to rip it clean off the wall. Instead he stuck the receiver in the refrigerator. It muffled most of the noise, but the cord kept the door from closing all the way, so Dylan took the receiver out again. With that damned siren still wailing, he ran into the living room, returned with a pillow, and buried the receiver in it. Peace at last.

Time agonized away. It had expanded beyond belief now, stretched out so that every second seemed like a minute, every minute a goddamned eternity.

Dylan kept staring at his watch, wishing, the way he often did near the end of a class period at school, that the minute hand would speed up and yet wishing that time would somehow stop altogether, or even reverse, and rescue his father. Finally he closed his eyes and lay back on the couch, utterly drained.

The next thing he knew, his mother was waking him from a deep, heavy sleep, letting him know with her eyes that it was time to go and—what would you call it? Check up on Al? See how he was doing? See if he was ready?

Dylan didn't really want to follow her upstairs, but he knew she wouldn't have the strength to go alone. In the hallway, they hesitated in front of the bedroom door. Then Kate forced herself to open it.

Dylan followed her inside. Except for the ticking of the clock, everything was still. The image burned itself into Dylan's memory: his father's expressionless lips, the bedspread's inappropriate cheer, the empty pill bottle and half-empty water glass sitting as witnesses on the nightstand. Kate hesitantly putting her fingers on Al's dangling wrist.

She looked at Dylan to confirm what they both already knew, and silently she began to sob, to shake, to weep. Dylan touched his father's lifeless face and then, shocked by the coolness of it, burst into tears himself. The ambulance would have to wait.

Chapter Fifteen

DYLAN went through the rest in a daze. Somehow he called the ambulance, somehow he watched it pull into the driveway, somehow he stood by as the attendants tried to revive his father. The doctor came and signed the death certificate. Two men from the funeral society carried the corpse away. The next time the doorbell rang, Barbra was standing there.

"What's going on?" she demanded. "You look horrible. And your phone's been busy all day. Are you okay?"

Dylan exhaled as though there were nothing left inside him but stale air. "Al's dead," he said, feeling as though it had taken him years to get the words out.

Barbra's expression collapsed. "When?"

"A couple of hours ago."

Barbra stood there gaping, shaking her head in disbelief. Then she moved forward and fell into Dylan's arms. He hugged her, supported her, let her cry on his shoulder. But who or what would support him?

The couch, at least. He led Barbra to it and they sat down. "He . . . he was fine Thursday," Barbra stammered, trying to control her tears. "I mean . . . you know, okay, not bad. How . . . how could it happen so fast?"

Dylan just stared at the tears streaming down her reddened cheeks. "How, Dylan?" she pleaded.

Oh, Christ, Al, why did you leave this to me, Dylan asked himself, especially now when I can barely even put one foot in front of the other, let alone think straight?

"How, Dylan?" Barbra repeated.

"How do you think?"

Looking him in the eyes, Barbra instantly caught his meaning, and Dylan knew there was no way he could hide anything from her. She could stare right into his brain cells. "No," she said firmly. "He wouldn't. He loved his life too much."

If you only knew, Dylan thought, if you only knew. If *I* only knew. Dylan couldn't hide the truth now, but how could he explain it, especially when he didn't want to believe it himself? How could he explain that Al had done what he wanted to, that nobody could stop him, that he had his own reasons that seemed to make sense when he was alive to explain them but now were as dead and useless as he was? "He did," Dylan said, sticking to the unvarnished, unpleasant fact.

"Why? Did he leave a note?"

Dylan shook his head.

"Didn't you even have a clue about it?" Her dark eyes were glistening with an intensity that Dylan couldn't bear. "Didn't you?" she repeated, tossing her long dark mane. Dylan looked away.

"Damn it, Dylan, say something!"

Yes, say something, damn it, get it over with, muttered a small voice through the layers of numbness and hangover and grief. It'll come out sooner or later. "He planned this for a long time."

At first the words didn't register. Barbra just sat there mute, perplexed, considering just what his remark could possibly signify. "You mean you knew? Ahead of time?"

How could he keep it from her?

"You knew and you didn't try to stop him?"

What did it matter now? Al was dead. He couldn't be hurt any more. But this was the woman Dylan loved, a person he didn't want to lie to. "We did try."

136

"You didn't tell *me*," she said, hurt and angry at the same time.

"He didn't want us to."

"Why? Why?"

Dylan shrugged numbly. "I tried to get him to tell you. He didn't think people would understand. He wanted to keep it in the family. He didn't want to hurt you."

"Didn't . . ."

It was pouring out now, Dylan couldn't stop it. "I asked him to say good-bye to you, but he wouldn't. Either he couldn't handle it, or he thought you couldn't, I don't know . . ."

Barbra bit her lip and sighed. "Then you knew he was going to do this today?"

Dylan fidgeted with his fingers.

"You mean you just sat there and let him kill himself?"

Dylan looked away. "Come on, it's bad enough that he's dead."

"Dylan, you could have saved him. He had a lot to live for."

Dylan shook his head. "This was how he wanted it. He wanted it this way." He looked up at Barbra, hoping she would believe him.

"He couldn't've, Dylan. He couldn't've," she repeated, and got up to leave.

Dylan followed her, wondering what he could say to her, wondering how he could make her understand at least what he understood, which, God knew, wasn't much. But the words wouldn't come. "What was it you said you wanted to talk to me about?" he blurted out in a last-ditch effort to bring her back. Barbra's only reply was to hurry out the door even faster. Dylan felt too weak to go after her. He could hear the Celica starting up with an angry roar and screeching away. He just hoped she would get home in one piece.

As he trudged up the stairs, he heard his mother sobbing in the bedroom. Al was right again, he thought bitterly: people wouldn't understand what he'd done. Dylan went into his bedroom and cried until it made his pillow soggy.

He slept the rest of the afternoon and all night. Sleep was thick, dull, dreamless, endless. The reality of the morning hit him hard. His surroundings looked the same—the *Revenge of the Surfer* poster on the wall, the books on the bookshelf, the keys on the dresser—but there was a hole in his life. He could somehow feel—not just know, but actually feel—that his father had gone, gone forever, and how nothing, no one, could take his place. The house hadn't changed at all, yet it was emptier, quieter, incomplete. As he poured himself some orange juice, Dylan half expected Al to come down the stairs for breakfast—yet at the same time, he knew it was impossible.

As the days went on, things got no better. It wasn't just Al's presence that was gone from the house. The fire chief hadn't been exaggerating at that testimonial dinner when he'd said that Al had courage enough for three people. In the past few months, Al *was* the courage for three people. If he were still around, he could give Kate and Dylan the strength to carry on. But his strength, like his body, was ash now, and there was nothing to replace it. Not friends: they meant well, but they didn't understand—not even Marco, who realized it had to have been suicide but just couldn't accept it—or if they did, they couldn't express their sympathy with anything more than the standard phrases, clichés, platitudes. Not relatives: his grandparents did understand, in their own way—Dylan was sure of it when he spoke with them on the phone—but they had their own personal pain and grief to deal with, and their reserves of sympathy were almost used up.

Worst of all, not Barbra, the only other person who knew the truth, or a lot of it, about Al's death. Barbra was the one person Dylan had expected to count on. After all, she'd been through something like this herself. But now she too had taken herself away. She didn't want to see him yet, she said when he phoned. She couldn't forgive him for not telling her about Al beforehand. She especially couldn't forgive him for not doing more to save his father. She needed time to think things over. She didn't want to see him, at least not now, not for a while.

So the hole in his life, already big enough to swallow him up, had grown deeper and wider, and Dylan was falling in. He and Kate could barely speak to each other about what had happened—at times they couldn't even bear to look at each other—so they stayed out of each other's way. They both just went through the motions of doing the things they absolutely had to, taking care of the will and the credit cards and the insurance and the other boring details as though they were sleepwalking.

If there was any joy in Dylan's life, he didn't feel it. Even his grief was dull, numb. Everything was empty, as hollow as the echoes of the Fourth of July fireworks he heard from his bed but didn't bother to go to see. Jay was away working as a camp counselor, Sean and Yolanda were busy with some sort of summer media course down in L.A., and Julie, not that he really wanted to see her, was running around with some guy who was home from college up north. Surfing was too much effort, people's radios bothered him at the beach, and hang gliding was out of the question. Dylan just kept shuffling through life, up to the Safeway for groceries, down to the bank for cash, onto the chaise longue for a nap. At dinnertime, out to the Colonel or McDonald's or the Pizza Port, since Kate didn't feel much like cooking. Or anything else. Mostly she just sat around doing nothing, except when she poured herself a drink.

Dylan kept hoping that all the answers would come, that he'd quit blaming himself for letting his father commit suicide, that he'd know why he didn't save him when all it would have taken was one lousy phone call, that somehow he'd understand everything, that it all would resolve itself in one great cosmic flash of insight. In the meantime he was desolate. He would phone Barbra half a dozen times a day. Usually there'd be no answer. Once in a while her father would pick up the phone and Dylan would leave a message, but Barbra never called back. And when she did answer, the conversation always seemed to be more or less the same:

BARBRA: Hello?

DYLAN: It's me.

BARBRA: Oh.

DYLAN: Can't we talk?

BARBRA: Dylan, I've told you. Please just leave me alone for a while. Okay?

DYLAN: No. It's not okay.

BARBRA: Good-bye, Dylan.

And then she'd hang up.

Sometimes, on those rare occasions when he had an extra supply of energy, he would try to force a conversation, ask her specifically what was wrong, what they could do to get back together, what he could do to make up with her. Sometimes he would remind her of how close they had been, ask her to understand what he was going through, remember how she felt when she lost her mother. Barbra would either go silent or hang up.

After the fifteenth (or was it, as it seemed, the fiftieth?) nonconversation, Dylan drove up to Meralta to confront her in person. There was nothing else left to do. As he turned off the freeway, he became uneasy, felt like an outsider the way he had the first time he'd gone up there. He *was* an outsider again, he realized, his one connection to Meralta cut off, all but vanished.

As he came up the drive, he noticed the Celica parked in front of the house. She was still home. She had to be. He rang the doorbell.

The little peephole became sort of flesh-colored. "Please go away, Dylan," said the pained voice from the other side. "I don't want to see you."

"Barbra, I have to talk to you."

"I don't have to talk to you."

"Look, it just doesn't make any sense," he said, wondering how you could make a peephole understand. "At least explain it to me. Or try to."

There was a long silence. "Please, Dylan," begged that quivering voice he knew so well. "Go away."

"Barbra, what's wrong, damn it? What the hell is wrong?"

There was another long silence. This time it was broken by the sound of the three locks opening. From behind the door, Barbra emerged, suspicious, defensive, wary. And particularly beautiful.

A stab of pain shot through Dylan's heart. "God, if you knew how I miss you," he blurted out.

"How are you?" she asked, her defenses visibly weakening.

"Guess," Dylan mumbled.

"Oh, God, this is so hard," she said, exhaling heavily.

"What is?"

Barbra took a deep breath, and Dylan braced himself. Whatever was coming, it wasn't likely to be good. And the way he felt, a marble could have bowled him over.

"You know what I said about being angry that you didn't do more to save Al? And that you kept it from me?"

Dylan nodded mechanically.

"Well . . . God, this is so hard . . . I was keeping something back from you, too. Not telling you something. I, uh . . . I fell in love with my sax teacher."

141

Dylan just stood there and let the news penetrate his numbness.

"He, uh . . . we're seeing each other," she said, her head wagging from side to side as though it wasn't held on quite right. "And . . . well, obviously, the whole thing happened in a big hurry. I haven't been taking those lessons that long. I wanted to tell you the day Al died—that's why I called that day, remember?—but afterward I couldn't get up the nerve. I guess I was a little bit in love with Al, too."

Dylan was totally stunned. He staggered back against the Celica. He felt as though it had run him over.

"I guess I was being selfish, thinking maybe the whole thing wouldn't work out or something and then you and I could get back together and everything would be okay again."

A dull, heavy weight pressed down on Dylan's brain, a stifling fog choked him. He thought he made some sound. He wasn't sure.

"I'm sorry," Barbra said, making no move toward him. "I feel terrible. I don't know what to say."

What else was there to say? How could anybody treat another human being this way? Somehow Dylan climbed into the Blazer, started it up, and threaded it down the drive, speeding out into the road without looking, making an oncoming driver swerve, swear, and honk.

It didn't faze Dylan a bit. He was utterly numb now, numb with rage, numb with pain upon pain upon pain. It had never happened to him before. He was the one who dropped people, not the other way around. And he did it, at least he tried to, with a little class, a little gentleness. All right, he'd been kind of rotten to Julie, but only after she'd turned into a real pain in the ass.

Now people were dropping him, or dropping out of his life, which amounted to the same thing. That hole in his existence was widening, deepening, growing limitless, bottomless, and there wasn't anything he could do to stop it. There wasn't anything he could do, period.

Yes, there was.

Chapter Sixteen

DYLAN lay back on his bed and stared up at the ceiling. For the first time since his father's death, he felt a tremendous inner peace, a calm that seemed to permeate his entire body. He was in control of his life again. He had all the answers. Al had been right. Suicide was—Dylan smirked at the pun— the way to go.

Dylan couldn't remember when he'd ever felt so much in control of his life. Now he knew exactly when it would be over: tomorrow morning at seven o'clock. He glanced at the calendar on the wall: after tomorrow, all the rest of the days would be useless. At least, to him.

He understood exactly how Al felt. Knowing exactly when he would die gave him power, strength. It let him rise above his pain, knowing every twinge of it would be destroyed with him the next morning when he'd take the glider high above the ledge and come plummeting down from the skies. A distinctive way to die. No pills, no bedspread: creative suicide for real.

The answers were coming now, not in that flash he'd been waiting for, but in a sort of tide, a series of waves that brought him seas of understanding as they came in, washed away layers of pain as they went out. He understood his father's crazy optimism in the face of death, understood what it was like to tell the old grim reaper himself that you'd beat him to the punch, that you weren't afraid of his infamous scythe. He understood what his father meant about all the little annoyances of life no longer having the power to bother him. What could Barbra mean to Dylan ten seconds after his heart stopped beating?

And he realized how difficult, probably impossible, it was to explain all that to the living. As he watched Kate fix dinner—in the last week or so she'd recovered enough to do that, at least, and to register for a summer class over at the city college, and to cut her liquor bill down to a fraction of what it had been —he wondered how it would hit her, this second blow, when she found out about it tomorrow morning. It wasn't fair to her, strictly speaking, yet was it any more unfair than what Al had done? Al's life was his own, after all, and so was Dylan's. Other people would just have to get along as best they could. It was too bad, but that was how it was. Nobody said life was fair.

On the other hand, Al had had the guts to say good-bye. That much courage wasn't in Dylan's makeup. He didn't dare try to say good-bye to Kate, and anybody else he might think of saying it to was either out of town or, like Barbra, out of the question. Was there anything else he should do before his death? Dylan couldn't think of much. He didn't have a will, but what did that matter? The only thing he owned that anybody would really want was his glider, and after tomorrow that would be just a mass of ripped fabric and tangled tubes. The rest of his stuff—clothes, books, records—was just stuff. There were his bicycle and his surfboard, which somebody like Jay could probably use, but then Jay was going to college in Iowa, which wasn't exactly Surf City, U.S.A. Besides, Kate would know best how to get rid of everything.

Dylan was lying on his bed, lost in his thoughts, when he heard Kate call him to the phone. He'd dimly heard it ring, but he couldn't imagine anyone would be calling him. He went into his parents' bed-

146

room—have to avoid that plural, he reminded himself, then realized he didn't have much time to form new habits—and picked up the phone. "Hello?"

"Dylan?" said the voice on the other end. Barbra. Dylan hesitated a moment, heard his mother hang up the extension.

"Dylan?" Barbra asked again.

"Yeah?" he said curtly.

"Listen, I just want to apologize for what I said this afternoon. Not what I said, really, but the way I said it."

"It's okay," Dylan said.

"I mean, you came up on me when I wasn't expecting it. I wanted to find another way of telling you, but I never got the chance."

"It's okay," Dylan said.

"Look, I just wanted to say that I still appreciate the times we've had, what you did for me. Really. More than you know. I still want to be friends, I mean, if you're willing."

"Okay," Dylan said.

"I know I haven't been fair to you. Maybe this thing with Delbert won't work out. I mean, he *is* a lot older and he lives way down in L.A. and everything. I just need some time."

"Sure," Dylan said.

"Dylan, you sound so cold. It doesn't have to be that way, really. We could still have fun together."

"Sure," Dylan said.

"I feel terrible. I know I must've hurt you this afternoon, and I just want to tell you I didn't mean to. Forgive me?"

"Why not?" Dylan said.

"Listen, I can understand how you must feel. Really. But I'm glad we got everything out in the open. And when you want to talk, I'll be here. I promise. Okay?"

"Okay," Dylan said.

"Really, Dylan, don't take this so hard. It's not the end of the world. You'll live."

That's what you think, Dylan said to himself. "Sure," he replied.

"Listen, take it easy," Barbra told him. "See you?"

"Yeah," Dylan said. "Sure."

The conversation was over. Yeah, he thought angrily as he hung up the phone—"friends." What a joke. Just wait till tomorrow. Friends!

When the alarm chirped at five in the morning, he awoke from one of the vivid, crystal-clear dreams that plagued him all night. He kept seeing his father out there on the ledge in the glider, taking off, floating up, and then, just as he was about to dive . . . the whole dream would begin again. Or else it would flash to Barbra's face, or Kate's, and then his own, lying on his parents' flowered bedspread, and *then* the dream would begin again, like an instant-replay machine gone haywire.

He dragged himself out of bed and went through his morning bathroom ritual, not that he needed to worry about tooth decay any more, just to help him wake up. As he stared at himself in the mirror, the idea of suicide became both easier and tougher to handle. Easier, because he was certain it was, as Al had said, the simplest thing in the world to kill yourself. Tougher because images kept coming back to him: his gliding, evenings with Barbra, days at the beach. But then those images of beauty would suddenly stop, and Dylan would see Al lying limp on the bedspread or Barbra slamming a door on him, and the pain of living would return and give him the resolve to die.

While he was tossing back a glass of orange juice in the kitchen, Kate came in. Oh, hell, he thought. Here it comes. "Dylan, what are you doing up at this hour?"

Come on, be nice to her. This is the last time you'll ever be able to. "Couldn't sleep."

"I heard your alarm."

"Yeah."

"Please don't go gliding."

He didn't want to go out with a lie, but what could he say? That he was going to be all right? That he wouldn't get hurt? "Look, I need to. If I don't do it, I'm going to forget how."

"Dylan, at least you could have told me."

"I didn't want to worry you."

"Will you be careful?"

"Look, you've seen me do this now. I'm always in complete control."

Kate threw up her hands in resignation. "All right," she said. "All right. We both have to start living again, I suppose. Just take care, please?"

He couldn't just stand there and let the moment go by. He moved toward his mother, put his arm around her, and kissed her tenderly on the forehead. "You take it easy, too," he said. But as he backed away, she gave him a proud, loving look that sent a shudder down his spine. This wasn't going to be as easy as he thought.

Out in the garage he loaded the glider into the Blazer and checked it over one last time. As usual, it was sticking a little way out the back window. As usual, the parts kit was sitting on the floor beside it. As usual, his helmet was tucked against the back of the seat. The only unusual thing was that he wouldn't be stopping to bring anybody along to pick him up at the bottom. Wouldn't be necessary.

He started up the Blazer and backed it out of the driveway. The deep blue early-morning sky was beginning to lighten a little, but the sun was still behind the mountains. It was going to be a beautiful day.

Inside Dylan's head, things weren't quite so pretty. That instant-replay machine had run amok. Scenes from the recent past appeared in slow motion, at normal speed, backward, from different angles. Worst of all, just as in his dreams, they kept coming back over and over. Al and Barbra duetting on "Body and Soul," Al and Kate at that picnic in the mountains, Barbra in that dress at her front door, Al dead on the bedspread, Al dead on the bedspread, Al . . . the flood of images wouldn't shut off. He tried to dam it up by concentrating on his driving, but the roads were deserted that early in the day, and he knew them by heart anyhow. Hoping for some distraction, he switched on the radio, but those loose thoughts rattling around in his head drowned it out.

Stick to the plan, he kept telling himself, stick to the plan. At the base of the hills, he pulled over to a phone booth outside a gas station that wasn't open yet. The images in his head gave way to a dull terror as he dialed a number and deposited thirty cents for three minutes please.

"Hello?" said a sleepy voice at the other end of the line.

Barbra. Not her father. Dylan exhaled in relief. "It's me," he said.

"Dylan, do you know what time it is?"

"Can you meet me up at the landing area?" Dylan asked urgently. "I'm going to fly."

"What, right now?"

"Yeah."

"Dylan, are you kidding? I mean, I know you're pissed off at me, but . . ."

"Listen, just get there, okay?"

There was a long silence at the other end of the line. Finally Barbra's voice cut through the static.

"I don't know, Dylan."

"Please?"

It was only one word, but Dylan put so much emotion into it that he convinced her. "All right," she said. "I've got to get dressed and everything. I'll meet you at your place."

"No, no, come to the landing area. I'm already halfway to the ledge."

"Dylan, are you all right?"

Dylan just grunted.

"Okay. I'll be there soon."

Dylan tried to say thanks, but he'd swallowed his voice. He hung up.

Well, now everything was set. Barbra would be there to watch him. Even though the mountains still hid the sun, the sky was promising the kind of sharp California light he'd seen in his dreams the night before. A fine day, he thought as he slammed the door to the Blazer. A perfect day. I couldn't ask for a better day to die.

Chapter Seventeen

DYLAN parked the Blazer and squeezed his eyes shut, hoping it might stop the flow of images parading through his brain. The images just intensified. He saw firemen's picnics from his childhood through games of catch with his father in the backyard through forest streams where his family had set up camp through Barbra's fingers on the keys of her sax, all superimposed on top of each other, layer upon layer, like an exercise in media class.

He opened his eyes. Concentrate, he told himself as he took the glider out of the truck. This is serious business. It's your life here, damn it, and your death. You're in control.

He was in control of the glider, that much was certain as he stood it on end and began setting up the flying wires. But the memories, the images, remained uncontrollable. He connected the king post to the keel wire, and there was Julie, looking up at him with that incredible boneheaded sweetness of hers, trying to understand. He spread the crossbar, and Julie melted into Barbra, her features intense to the point of fierceness. As the sail rippled in the breeze, Barbra dissolved into Kate, who looked angry and hurt. Wincing, Dylan set his jaw and concentrated on the glider.

Yet there was nothing to concentrate on, his fingers having done this so many times they were working mechanically, so the images kept dancing in his head. Al was taking over now, Al and his laughter, Al and his philosophy, Al and his fire engine, Al and his medals. The lukewarm body on the brightly flowered bedspread. The empty pill bottle. The ambulance. The footprints disappearing in the sand.

As Dylan twisted the turnbuckles, the glider began to come alive in his hands. The wires tautened and twanged like giant guitar strings, and the sail's exuberant colors brought back the day he'd been given the glider, Al's look of pure delight in knowing he'd done something Dylan would enjoy. Then, by some peculiar trick of memory, Dylan saw his own face that day, his eyes glowing with gratitude and love, and fleetingly felt that long-ago tingle of happiness run across his skin. Where had that joy gone, he wondered, remembering how he'd found it for an instant, heavily mixed with sadness, the day he'd flown for his father. How could he ever recapture it now, when everything had turned to shit?

The inner torrent of sounds and images was separating him from the outside world, yet Dylan's fingers automatically fastened the connections on the glider, his eyes automatically checked and okayed them. And when the fingers and eyes had done their job, his glands automatically sent a jolt of adrenaline coursing through him. In his throat and his heart and his gut he felt it was time to get started. But he also felt a tidal wave of raw emotion that made his knees buckle.

Concentrate, concentrate, he told himself, trying not to weep. All I need is to overlook one wire, and this whole thing turns into a very bad joke. Instead of killing myself, this damned wing will do it for me.

His senses went on automatic once more as he ran through the safety check he'd memorized so well. Concentrate, concentrate, Dylan told his pounding heart as he went to the edge and looked down on the deeply shadowed hills.

"Concentrate, concentrate," he said out loud, but the noise inside his head was deafening, the collection of images blinding, his pulse overwhelming. Where was she, where was she? He kept trying to find Barbra down below, beneath the dozens of images heaped up in his vision.

Then a glint in the distance cut through his brain fog like a scalpel. It was the silvery gleam of the metallic doorposts on Barbra's Celica, flashing out as the car hurtled through the sunbeams.

She was here. She was turning up the road to the clearing. Dylan walked the glider back, ran forward without even thinking about it, and dived from the cliff.

The sail's holding. Concentrate, concentrate. Get to that thermal. Concentrate. Concentrate. Let it take you up. Concentrate.

Now hover. Wait.

The car door's opening. (Watch that little crosswind.) She's getting out. (Easy, easy.) She's looking around. (So small from up here.) She's looking up. (Keep looking, keep looking . . .) She sees.

She sees.

Now!

Dive!

Dive for keeps. Pull, pull, hold, hold, concentrate, concentrate, down, damn it, down! Don't fight me, that's right—down!

Down down hold down down hold downdowndown downdown

What in hell is that? Pink thing? Huge. Waving. My heart. For her birthday. I LOVE YOU. *Why?*

She was going to give it back she was going to make up with me she was trying to save me which damn it which?

I want to see how this comes out!

Concentrate! Concentrate! Push! Push! Slow up, damn you, slow up!

I want to see how this comes out!

Up! Out of the dive! Push! Up! Yes, that's . . . damn it, there's the

ground. Dylan felt a thud, heard aluminum cracking all around him. He was lying on his stomach, his left arm bent weirdly behind him.

I hurt, his arm told him. Do not move me. His legs, numb, said nothing. I do not want to die, Dylan told himself.

"I'm coming! I'm coming!" It was Barbra's voice screaming in the distance.

I want to see how this comes out.

A wave of nausea suddenly flowed through him, a wave of insight that flatly told him all those other waves of "understanding'" had been bummers, like those waves when you first learn to surf that look like they'll give you a good ride and then break right under you. Fakoes, phony thermals. What he'd taken for understanding, he now understood, was only the romance of death, that bastardly grim reaper dressed up to look sexy. He could hear Barbra's feet trampling the dry brush in irregular snaps as she came closer.

I want to see how this comes out.

How could he have confused himself with his father? Al was a completely different story. Al might have been right to kill himself. He also might have been wrong. He might have been both: right, for himself, and wrong for what he'd done to the people he left behind. Right, wrong, or both, he was Al, not Dylan. He wasn't just in pain, he was dying: he knew—or thought he knew—just how and when his story would come out.

But for Dylan to kill himself was like walking out early on the movie of his life. There was no way in hell he could know what the ending would be. "*You asshole!*" his mind screamed at him. He'd fucked up again, the same way he had on his ninth-grade assignment. Sure, it's your own life, asshole, but it's your own life only as long as you live it. *"ASSHOLE!"*

"Dylan! Dylan!" Barbra shrieked, leaning down and putting a hand on his cheek. "Don't move."

I want to see how this comes out.

He shifted his eyes to look at her. She was wearing a pink top, pink jeans. Through those layers of images, maybe he hadn't seen that birthday card. Maybe he'd just imagined it. Maybe she was the birthday card. Maybe she wasn't even there.

I want to see how this comes out.

"Can you say something?" Barbra asked softly. "Are you all right?" She had that look of concern, of caring, that Dylan knew so well, loved so much. He could barely see it now through his tears and stupidity and frustration and pain.

"I'll live," he said.

STEPHEN MANES is a versatile and popular author and screenwriter who has published more than a dozen books, including SLIM DOWN CAMP, BE A PERFECT PERSON IN JUST THREE DAYS! and THE BOY WHO TURNED INTO A TV SET. Mr. Manes lives in Riverdale, New York.

FLARE ORIGINAL NOVELS
By FANNY HOWE

THE BLUE HILLS   78998-1 $1.95

Aunt Bonnie has always been a mother to 13-year-old tomboy Casey Quick, after Casey's mother died and father went away. Then, one day, Casey learns that her aunt has gone away—and Casey, knowing Bonnie would never leave her without saying goodbye, doesn't know what to do. In her fear and confusion, she runs off to The Stables, near the Blue Hills outside of Boston where she can begin the search for her aunt. Willie, a tall, handsome 15-year-old who hangs around the stables, helps her and they develop a special friendship. When Casey finds out what has happened to Bonnie, she realizes the difference between true friends and false ones, and between dependence and love.

YEAH, BUT   79186-2 $1.95

In this sequel to THE BLUE HILLS, Casey is thrilled when she, her aunt and new uncle move into a luxurious condominium in Boston. But her boyfriend, Willie, thinks she is acting different about her new status and decides that she's "too young" for him. Liking her new home but missing her old friends, Casey tries to make new ones and learns that most people aren't what they seem. She still misses Willie and contrives a plan to win him back!

AVON 🖤 FLARE Paperback

Available wherever paperbacks are sold, or directly from the publisher. Include 50¢ per copy for postage and handling; allow 6-8 weeks for delivery. Avon Books, Mail Order Dept., 224 West 57th St., N.Y., N.Y. 10019.

Howe 8-82